Merman Rises

M.S. Kaminsky

Published by Open Pollinated Productions LLC

Special Thanks

To my family, my husband and to anyone who has ever felt they did not belong.

With special thanks to my extraordinary advance readers, Nina Gregor and my editor Tracy Seybold.
I could not do this without you!

mkaminsky.com

Chapter One - Delphin

MY NAME IS Delphin. A web as tangled as sea floss led to this moment. A moment where I drift deep beneath the sea, ready to record this story shell. The strange events that brought me here started in my pod, long before I'd ever met a human. Are you ready for my story?

* * *

If I'd lived the rest of my life and never witnessed an execution, that would have been fine by me.

Two of Father's fiercest merrow soldiers led Barron toward his death. Head bowed toward the seafloor, he swam between them. I tried to read the expression on his handsome face. Anger? Sadness? Resignation?

An enormous throng of merrow swam behind, buzzing with excitement. A rainbow assortment of fins glimmered and sparkled in the eerie light of the abandoned crystal caverns.

I glanced over and noticed my father, Jahvo, watching. I struggled to keep my emotions hidden, frozen behind an impassive mask.

Guilt soured my stomach. Shame slithered through my veins. Grief shattered my soul. I did not want to be here. I did not want to witness Barron's death! I had no choice. I was the regent's son.

Barron had been well-respected once. Just a few years older than me, he had a broad chest made strong from combat, eyes that twinkled with his quirky, self-deprecating sense of humor, and he wielded his trident with a dexterity that rivaled Father's most loyal soldiers, Finner and Teomath.

Now Barron will die. Because of me.

For a moment, Barron's eyes met mine. My throat constricted. I

1

forced myself to meet his gaze, expecting accusation or anger. But I saw nothing. Just a brief flicker of recognition before he glanced away.

I am a murderer.

My stomach roiled, and I almost threw up my shrimp breakfast. According to Father, Barron was not worthy of being sacrificed to our Tentacle Lord. Instead, they dragged him into the old forbidden zone to meet his fate. Merrow taunted and jeered.

Massive arches inlaid with ornate artistic flourishes towered above seaweed-covered statues and broken ornamentation. I'd never swam here before. These abandoned areas were where the decadence of the old merrow ways had been born and died.

This massive room looked so different from the austere chambers of our pod, which were all white, white, white. We'd risen above the old ways to create something better. Something pure. So I thought.

Finner forced Barron down to the seafloor. Teomath yanked his muscular arms, binding them behind him with thick ropes made from kelp and seaweed. Blood oozed from several puncture wounds on Barron's lustrous cobalt and gold fin. A giant chunk of a stone statue loomed above. His death sentence.

This room once held many statues. Now statues were forbidden. Art was banned. One of the thousand rules that governed our tribe.

Forty merrow pushed the statue closer to the edge of the ancient ledge. A horrible grinding noise shook the chamber and rattled my bones.

As they continued to shove the massive chunk of stone toward the edge, Barron's green-blue eyes met mine. A deep sadness emanated from him.

I felt Barron try to warn me of something, but I didn't dare open my mind to his transmission. Father watched. If I lost control, I'd lose everything. As it was, I barely managed to maintain the stoic mask that held back an ocean of sorrow.

I glanced up when the horrible grinding noise ceased. All the merrow went silent. The stone tipped and fell. It landed with a boom that launched an enormous plume of brown sediment.

A sharp stab of pain sliced through my chest. Barron lay crushed beneath.

* * *

Months later, in nightmares, Barron's eyes still floated in front of me.

What had he wanted to tell me?

The pain in my chest faded. It never left. An echo of that day. Most times when I had aches or pains, I visited Abalon, our healer. She grew hundreds of sea herbs and remedies for all kinds of ailments.

Not this time.

After what I'd done to Barron, I deserved whatever punishment I got. In fact, I deserved far worse.

Chapter Two - Delphin

ON SPAWNING DAYS, there were no rules. I burrowed deeper into the soft, colorful folds of sea-silk and tried to hide.

Color was permitted in this chamber but nowhere else. Silks were hand-woven from cultivated seaweeds and dyed beautiful oranges, greens, and yellows. Any other day, I'd have enjoyed their beauty. Right now? Fear muddled my brain.

When other young mermen my age learned of the lack of rules, they pumped their fists in the air, giant grins on their faces.

Their glee bewildered me. *No rules? Why celebrate that?*

It seemed a horrible idea that invited chaos. I'd learned to navigate our rules. I knew what to expect. There were no surprises.

Peeking through a gap in the silks, I watched Crusock and Sirena pass hand-in-hand. Sirena giggled. Crusock nipped the nape of her neck.

Crusock had bullied me since I was a fry. I wasn't surprised to see him with Sirena. She'd always been a sucker for muscle heads. They drifted into silk love nest in a flurry of bubbles and hands. Touching, stroking, caressing.

I shut my eyes and took a deep breath of water. Barron's face flashed in my mind. I saw the stone descend.

That could be you next.

No. I have my plan.

I hoped Krenil was right. Our plan felt solid when we'd talked it through. Now it felt as fragile as minnow bones. I ran it through my mind for the umpteenth time.

I'd tell Father I fell asleep in the sea-silk. I'd explain that my excitement about the spawning the night before took its toll. It wasn't that I hadn't *wanted* to spawn. I'd passed out from sheer exhaustion.

4

My father's advisor, Krenil, told me there was another way I could become an initiate. Without spawning. He hadn't gone into specifics but that was my out.

I'd dreaded this day for several moons. Krenil assured me it would go better than expected. Wrong. It was about to get worse. Much, much worse.

A hand shot through the folds of sea-silk and smacked my backside hard enough to sting.

"I thought I heard you!" Chrysalis was one of the older, more experienced mermaids and now she'd found me. I'd tried to cloak my thoughts, but that was not one of my strong points. Especially when I got nervous.

Father had encouraged her advances at our last Regent's dinner. In fact, he seemed to find my discomfort humorous. Chrysalis made bawdy jokes that made me blush and finned me under the table. My sister theorized that she wanted the power I might hold one day. I was more pragmatic: Chrysalis wanted nothing more than to eat me alive.

Chrysalis ran her hands along my chest down to my belly. I thrust my tail down in the sandy surface that lay beneath the undulating sea-silk and rocketed out into the maze of passages. Okay, she might have found me, but she hadn't caught me—yet.

On spawning days, there were no rules.

That meant there was no rule that said I needed to make it easy for her! Perhaps time would run out before she caught me? I swam hard and fast. If she did catch me, I could blow my whistle, though Krenil told me it was a last resort.

There were laws, rules, and regulations for everything in our pod. Rules for when and what we could eat. They regulated sleeping times; half the pod slept during the moon, the other half during the sun except during celebrations—this was for safety.

Other regulations dictated what we wore and when. In the many passages that crisscrossed our pod, mermaids swam to the left, mermen to the right. I didn't know the purpose of this—it just was. There were regulations about when we could enter the open sea—never except during the Hunts, which only happened twice per year for certain initiated merrow.

Hunts were another example when there were few rules—not no rules, but few enough to make me uncomfortable. When I became Regent, I'd banish Hunts, although I hadn't mentioned this to Father.

Rules kept us safe. Regulations kept us secure. Laws kept things certain. Most of all, order kept us alive.

My mind ran through escape routes as I gathered speed during a long, straight stretch of open water. Chrysalis swam close behind, laughing.

"Oh, how fun you are, cheeky Delphin!" She squealed with another burst of laughter. "You know I love a challenge."

Most of the other mermaids and mermen had already paired off. I zoomed past a few—grunts and guttural sounds rose from sea-silk nests.

My sense of direction was horrible. Lost, I barreled through the maze of sea-silk and careened down a dead-end. I took a sharp left, then a right, zigzagging back-and-forth. My hesitation cost momentum. Chrysalis gained.

"Sweet Delphin! So frisky! So cheeky!" Her laughter and giggles followed close behind. "So speedy!" She sent out a probe, seeking my thoughts. I barricaded fast but not before she caught a glimpse. *Damn it.*

"You poor thing!" she transmitted. "You are nervous."

We merrow communicated to each other by transmitting mind-to-mind. It's not that different from human speech. Well, except for one thing. It's also possible to read a merrow's mind if you're rude enough to breach their defenses.

My heart hammered in my throat. Nervous? Try terrified. I needed some way out of this predicament. Perhaps a little known dictate, edict, or precept? Anything. But I came up empty. Rules and regulations would not help me now.

I remembered Krenil's advice. Krenil was more a father to me than my own. Although I couldn't tell him the whole truth, it was he to whom I'd confided my fears.

"Well, if you get found in your comfy hideaway, then blow your mother's whistle," Krenil said with a suppressed smile. "I will make an excuse and come call you away on urgent business."

"The Hall of Order is so vast and far away," I'd said. Krenil spent most of his time there. It was all the way on the other side of the network of passages I called home.

Krenil's droopy eyelids had opened and closed. He tapped the bone whistle that hung around my neck. It didn't look like anything special. A piece of rudimentary carved bone on a rough-hewn seaweed rope necklace. I only wore it because it reminded me of my mother.

"No worries, lad. Your mother's whistle was made from the larynx of a Trillium Whale. One could hear their calls throughout the seven seas and beyond. That is until they went extinct, thanks to humans. Blow. I will find you no matter where you are. But only whistle as a last resort, mind you. It will put me in a somewhat awkward position."

Chrysalis had a single goal: to initiate me and make me hers before the next moon. Before the most important Hunt of the year, all young men of age needed to be initiated. Part of me hoped that somehow as I spun, twisted, and turned throughout the maze of sea-silks, that she'd tire. From the shrieks of delight coming from behind me, Chrysalis enjoyed the chase.

I swam so hard I thought my head might pop like a pufferfish. When I dared take a quick look behind me, I'd lost her. I slowed. If I hadn't, my heart might have burst right out of my chest. I drifted a bit and when I looked up, Chrysalis swam right in front of me. I tumbled into her waiting arms and she grabbed me and pulled me close.

"Got you!" she screamed as her mouth opened and her tongue penetrated my lips.

"Your heart beats so fast. Don't be scared." Chrysalis snapped my upper lip with her teeth, drawing blood. I grabbed for my whistle but before I could put it to my bleeding mouth, she wrapped her thick arms around my torso, her grip tightening. Something in my chest cracked.

"This is supposed to be fun, silly. Relax."

Fun? She might eat me alive!

"I'll be more gentle." She nuzzled against me and gyrated her body back and forth against mine. Her breasts pressed against me like two giant loaves of sea sponge bread. I squirmed beneath her as I tried to pull my right hand up to my chest to grab the whistle.

"Mmm, yes, more. It feels soooo good when you do that." Chrysalis moaned so deep a trail of hairs rose along the nape of my neck.

She reached down. I tried to jerk back but her hand darted beneath my waist and reached to grab... nothing. Only water. My parts remained retracted. Hidden within my body. Could you blame them?

"Oh!" Surprise and anger clouded her face. She shoved me away. "I thought you enjoyed my company!" Her mouth curled in a snarl.

"How could you *possibly* think that?" I said without thinking first. Seeing the flash of rage in her eyes, I tried to backtrack.

"I mean, it's not you... I just... sorta... tired out." I managed a garbled, disjointed mind-to-mind transmission.

"No need for excuses. I understand." She flung her hair over her shoulder. The water around her practically boiled. She swam away, then turned. "Oh, and, Delphin? You don't need to worry, my sweet. I won't mention your… performance to anyone."

Chrysalis shot me a sarcastic wink and swam off into the sea-silk maze.

Chapter Three - Delphin

I PANICKED. NOT wanting to see anyone, I rushed through unused back corridors on my way to find Krenil.

Blackened slime-covered crystal walls surrounded me on all sides. Father's improvement mandates left these for last. They were not yet plastered with the smooth white material that covered most of our chambers. These dark, narrow passages were used to transport building materials and for servants. They circled the main areas.

My sister, Ariella, told me that the crystal had been beautiful once. Hard to imagine. Many things had changed since the old times, generations before my sister and I were born.

Tango, my pet dolphin, found me and followed. He'd been perplexed that he hadn't been allowed to enter the spawning room. His cool, slick, blue bottlenose nudged itself up beneath my armpit.

"That tickles, Tango! Quit it!" He knew how to get a laugh out of me. Even when there was nothing to laugh about.

After Barron's execution, we'd explored the forbidden areas of our pod and discovered an abandoned palace. Admittedly, it was much more fun to hang out there.

We'd found a garden of story shells. Each colorful shell held its own story, as diverse as they were beautiful. Ariella listened to one about the human world that existed above the seas. She'd been obsessed with it ever since.

"Delphin?" A familiar voice. Ariella shot a pulse of echolocation, our way of using sounds waves to see. I spotted her collecting conch shells in a shadowy recess. "I've been looking for you." She grinned. "Ready for more exploration?"

"No. Enough. I can't go there again. It's against the rules. Besides, I need to find Krenil. It's urgent."

She swam out and bumped me playfully with her tail. "C'mon, you know you want to. Maybe you'll find another story shell?"

Ariella's face broke out into a broad smile. She rolled over onto her back and swam in front of me, her long silver hair exploding around her face. Despite her large size or perhaps because of it, Ariella was the most graceful swimmer I'd ever seen. I was biased. Ariella was not only my sister but also my best friend.

"What happened to your lip? It's bleeding."

"Chrysalis happened." I filled my sister in, along with Krenil's promise to help.

Ariella rolled her eyes at Krenil's name. "Delph, don't worry about Chrysalis. Love won't bend to rules. Rules will harden your heart until it shatters into a billion pieces!"

"I will never fall in love." *Again,* I almost said but stopped myself. "And even if I did, no one will ever love me back. It's pointless."

She stroked my cheek. "I love you, brother. You and I are alike. We deserve true love but one never to be found down here, it seems. Tell Father that Chrysalis misunderstood. He's preoccupied with the next Hunt. Now let's forget our troubles and explore."

"He commanded that I *go* on my first Hunt! This year I must. Much younger mermen have already hunted."

She grimaced. "Ugh, Hunts. Barbaric, boring and a waste of energy." Ariella was built large for a mermaid her age. She had no patience for strenuous exercise.

"Come, Delphin." She swam around me in big, looping figure-eights. "A story always puts you in a happier state of mind."

I shook my head. "Ariella, you're making me dizzy! Seriously, this is bad." I had to find Krenil. Chrysalis had looked furious. "I need his advice. Everyone leaves *you* alone. Not me. I'm already a target."

Being the regent's son made life very difficult for a merman different from the rest.

Ariella folded her arms and pouted. "Fine. Krenil will be no help, but try. I'll tell you what you missed out on later."

She swam off into the darkness. I watched her go for a moment and then thrust hard with my fin as I headed in the opposite direction.

Without Ariella around to distract me, what happened with Chrysalis played over and over. Arms trailing behind me, I swam as fast as my fin could propel me through the corridors.

Tango nudged me from behind. We had a game he liked to play. I grabbed his dorsal fin and pushed while he pulled me. Together, we zoomed through the water faster than any fish or merrow I'd ever seen.

* * *

Where else would I find Krenil, except the Hall of Order? Eighty percent of the pod spent much of each day here. They ground up calcium coral and seaweed cement. Workers smoothed over the old crystal walls with pure white plaster.

In the Hall of Order, Krenil engraved the walls with long, red scrawls of rules and regulations that governed our pod. When I arrived, he was scolding two apprentices.

"Remember, it will cure fast in the saltwater. Be more efficient, Sera! Stop darting back-and-forth. I'd better find a smoother surface when I return." He glanced over and saw me. His eyes twinkled, and he broke away from his workers, guiding me to a quiet corner.

"You, shoo! Getaway!" He shook his fist at Tango, who was nosing around for shrimp. Pets weren't common. In fact, I was the only merman who had one. Tango had a particular fondness for the ground-up shrimp Krenil used to make his red ink.

"Go," I told Tango with a gentle pat on his belly.

Tango flitted off down the corridor.

"Young master, did all go as planned? Are you aware that your top lip is twice the size of the bottom? You look like a clownfish!" He chuckled.

"Never mind my stupid lip." I grabbed his shoulders. "Chrysalis found my hiding place, and it went badly. She was offended that I was... too tired to spawn with her. She'll tell everyone. Father will find out. Can you talk to Chrysalis?"

Krenil scratched his pointy, gray-whiskered chin and closed his eyes. "I can talk to her, yes."

"What about my initiation? You mentioned a rule... or was it a loophole? Some way I might still go on the Hunt without it? Father commanded me to go this time!" Krenil had kept me clear of my father's wrath on many occasions. This time, it would not be easy.

"Easy, young sir, calm yourself." Krenil patted my shoulder. "A longer face I've never seen." A crooked smile flashed across his face. "Ah, here look! No wonder you had such trouble with Chrysalis." He snatched an object from my ear and held it out in front of me.

Sitting in the center of his palm lay a fat, pink shrimp. "You had a shrimp stuck in your ear all this time!"

A smile cracked my face. Krenil had amused Ariella and me with his sleight-of-hand tricks since we were fry.

Krenil played with his whiskers. "Now as I said, I came across a dictate that *may* help you in your situation. In fact, it may help a great deal."

"Will it involve Chrysalis?"

Krenil popped the shrimp in his mouth and crunched it. He smacked his lips and shook his head. "Don't worry about her. I need to research a couple of things. Have you put in a good word for me to Ariella yet?"

Krenil had a massive crush on Ariella. Feelings that Ariella did not share in the least. Somehow, I'd gotten stuck in the middle. If Krenil thought anyone could change Ariella's mind, he didn't know her well.

"I mentioned your interest." I turned to study the scrawling whorls of inscribed rules, regulations, and dictates as if they were suddenly the most fascinating things in the world.

"And?" Krenil grabbed my arm and forced me to look at him.

My face reddened to the color of the shrimp he'd just eaten. Ariella's response had been peels of mirthful laughter. With enormous effort, I shielded my thoughts.

Krenil waved me off. "Fine, fine. I'll talk to her myself. Meet me on your way to trident practice tomorrow. I'll fill you in on what you might do to initiate."

Chapter Four - Elias

RAYS OF GOLDEN sun lit up the mosque across the dusty road as Elias hefted water from the old well. Returning to his family's kitchen, the tangy smell of za'atar and tomato filled his nose.

Inside, Elias' father, Oren, sat cross-legged on a floor cushion waiting for lunch. His mother, Inas, stirred chickpeas in a metal pot while his sister, Nijah, cut tomatoes, bangs draped over her high forehead.

Oren slammed the ancient wooden table with his hairy fist at the climax of a familiar tale. A story Elias had heard over and over since he could remember.

"The pain, you can't imagine, it was incredible! Enormous!" Oren yanked his pant leg up to his knee. "How I made it those next three miles, Mama? I can't even fathom." He gestured toward a long scar Elias had seen a thousand times.

"Timu thinks he's some hero? He's just a kid. What good will he do? We need real men fighting for the motherland. Like your great-grandfather. Like me!" Father thumped his rotund chest. Mom emitted a sympathetic *tsk* and nodded—the ever-supportive audience.

It was Saturday. Oren wore granddad's jewel-encrusted leather sheath at his side. His grandfather had fought in the Seventh's War. The knife was stolen decades ago. Oren had never found a replacement to fit the sheath's odd, curved shape. Despite that, he wore the empty sheath each Saturday in honor of the man.

Elias forced himself to stay quiet, but it was difficult. How dare Oren compare himself to Timu? Timu!?

"I'd rain fire on those sons of bitches! If I had my health, by god, things would be different in Fahad. There's no order to what they're doing. Mama, I heard they're headed west. West! If I were

13

commandant..."

Biting into a wrinkled, black olive, Elias savored it, allowing the rich, salty flavor to flood his mouth and drown out the rant. It was their last jar. Maybe it would be the last olive he'd ever taste? If they didn't take action, it might be. Most families had fled weeks ago.

Elias' family sat cross-legged around the low table, as they shared a meal of flatbread, roasted chickpeas, canned olives, and diced tomatoes Inas had gathered from their neighbor's dying garden. Soon they'd run out of food. Rather than figure out what action to take, Father droned on about past glories.

Elias thought of Timu and felt a swell of pride. They'd lost touch over the months, headed in different directions. It was a fact of life that bothered him. He missed Timu even though their arrangement couldn't have lasted. Or could it? Not for Timu. If things had been different, maybe. Another life. Now Timu was at war. At eighteen, just two years older than him.

After dinner, his father slumbered, having eaten twice what any of them had. Elias helped Nijah and Inas clean. A year ago, they'd lived in a comfortable white-washed building near the park. A courtyard led to a tidy garden that overlooked a small vineyard bursting with grapes.

Now their home consisted of patched concrete walls, a tin roof, and no running water. Desert winds blew a steady supply of dust and debris. The whole family had developed chronic coughs and wore scarves around their faces whenever they spent time outside.

"Could you talk to Timu?" Inas whispered to Elias while he chiseled hardened rice from a dented stainless steel pot. No matter what happened, her pale, pink lips always curved up into a slight, peaceful smile. Although, it seemed every day another gray hair sprouted on her head.

The distant sound of artillery echoed off the buildings. Elias wasn't sure what bothered him more, that such sounds came with increasing regularity or that they no longer fazed him. So far, they'd been lucky. That is to say, they weren't dead. Yet. Many from their village *had* died. The longer they stayed, the greater the chance their luck would end.

"What can Timu do for us?" Elias whispered. "Father spoke to him twice."

"Father did most of the talking, I think," she said with a wry smile.

Elias nodded. Father's idea of speaking to Timu had been to give him advice. To lecture him. To spew jealousy that a man—just a boy! —

so much younger could lead a troop, however rag-tag.

"You could try," Inas said.

Elias nodded. "We were good friends once." He blushed. Maybe he'd said too much, but Inas didn't notice. "I will. I'll go find him this afternoon."

"It can't do any harm… Just… be careful. How will you find him?" Another explosion.

Elias gestured over his shoulder. Wherever there was the sound of chaos and gunfire, Timu was sure to be nearby.

Inas grabbed him. "Not now. Wait a few days until the fighting dies."

"Mother…"

His resolve wavered, bravery leaking out into the soft comfort of his mother's arms. No! He would not become his father. Back straight, he pushed his mother away.

"I'm not some little boy, you know. I'm just two years younger than Timu!" At that, he felt a pang of guilt return. Like father, like son. Why wasn't *he* fighting with Timu? One of Timu's soldiers was around his age. But the truth was he didn't want to stay and fight. What he wanted was to lead his family to safety, to get them out of this hell.

* * *

Wrapping a bandana around his mouth against the dust, Elias headed out into a smoky, dusty afternoon. Darting from one abandoned dwelling to another, he noticed that there were many more families hidden in the ruins of his town than he'd realized.

He didn't recognize their faces. Things must have gotten worse to the east. If their forlorn town offered more opportunities than where these people had come from, well, that was terrifying.

Elias shut his eyes against a sudden blast of sand in the dry, hot wind. Although confident that he'd find Timu, he wasn't sure if Timu would speak privately, let alone help. Their friendship had ended badly.

Thinking back, he couldn't have seen it working out differently. At the time, he'd have sacrificed plenty to keep their secret meetings. Then the war came. Now, none of that mattered.

A swift kick to his legs sent him sprawling to the ground, biting a mouthful of dirty sand. Rough hands rolled Elias over onto his back. A man in a dirty gray bandana pinned his arms, searching for weapons.

"I'm local! I'm from Farad!" Elias hoped the man recognized his accent with his mouth half full of dirt.

The guy finished checking his pockets and let him stand, eyeing him. "What are you doing creeping around the front? I almost shot you. Are you here to fight?"

"I need to see Timu."

"Timu?" he asked. "Why would Timu see you?"

"I know him. He's a friend. We went to the same school." His chest tightened as he remembered Timu's last, harsh words to him. *We aren't friends. I don't know you. You don't know me. Now I never wanna see you again. Got it?*

The man insisted on blindfolding Elias. He forced him through a maze of broken buildings. He knew they were broken because he kept smashing the toes of his sandals into crumbled pieces of brick and drywall. After several minutes, he got shoved into a dark room and the blindfold was ripped from his face.

Timu's face stayed neutral when their eyes met. Not a flicker of recognition. It felt surreal to remember the time they'd shared, hidden in an abandoned shed. Timu leaned back against a rusty metal table, arms folded. Several other young guys in dirty muscle-shirts hunched over beat-up laptops and cobbled-together radio equipment.

Elias opened his mouth to speak but didn't know what to say. Timu was even more handsome than he remembered. He no longer looked like a teen. His chest and arms rippled with muscle. His jaw was a sharp line of pure willpower.

What left Elias sputtering was not the attraction that still smoldered for the rebel fighter. It was Timu's menacing air. He looked mean. Dangerous. His eyes were those of a man who had killed and would kill again. Even though he fought on their side, for his family, for their village, it left him chilled.

Timu jerked his head toward a small room to his left. "Put him in there. I'll deal with him in a minute."

Deal with me?

Elias got shoved into a dank storeroom filled with plastic water containers and boxes of cornflakes. The door slammed, locking him in. A few minutes later, Timu entered, alone, and shut the door with a soft click.

"What are you doing here?" Timu asked, his voice soft but dangerous. "Did you forget what we agreed?"

"No." Elias struggled to keep the resentment from his voice. "We need help, my family. We're running out of food. Everyone else has left for the port. It's only refugees here now. If we don't get out soon…"

"You'd abandon the motherland so easily?"

"Timu, please. We aren't fighters. You know my father… and I'm not cut out for it." Elias reached out and put his hand on Timu's bare arm. Timu flinched and jerked his arm back.

It was quick, fleeting, but he felt certain he'd seen a flash of pain cross Timu's face. He pressed his advantage, however brief. Elias took a step closer until they stood a few feet apart. They were close enough that Elias could have leaned out and pressed their bodies together. A year ago, he would have.

"Please," Elias said, voice catching in his throat. He grabbed Timu's hand. This time, his friend hesitated before he pulled away. Timu's eyes flashed with anger. He shoved Elias as hard as he could.

Elias hit the stone wall with a dull thud and slid to the dirty floor, gasping for air. Timu yanked Elias up to his feet, fists burning against Elias' bare chest.

"You're even stronger than I remember." Elias put his hand on Timu's sweaty forearm.

They paused there for a moment.

"Timu?" he whispered.

Timu pulled his right fist back and punched Elias in the face while his left hand held him in place for another blow. Elias fell to the floor, curled up against the onslaught.

When Elias arrived home, bloody and beaten, his mother ran to him.

"Oh, my poor son!" Inas grabbed Elias by his shoulders. "Nijah! Boil some water! Were you ambushed?"

Elias shook his head. "Timu arranged a truck for us. We're leaving."

Chapter Five - Delphin

THE NEXT DAY, Tango swam beside me as I headed to trident practice. For the third time, my dolphin companion stopped to scratch his flank against the rough, white-hewn walls.

"Tango, what's wrong with you today? You're making *me* itchy."

Nervous, I twirled my trident and passed it from my right to left hand, accidentally dropping it to the tunnel floor, as white as bone and just as hard.

My head darted to the left and then the right. Bad start to a morning of trident drills! A merman was *never* to drop his trident. Luckily, no one was around.

My mind wasn't on our drills. I wanted to find Krenil and learn what he had to tell me. My stomach clenched as I entered the main corridors and swam past other merrow.

"Good day," Abalon said as she swam past. She was our healer.

"Good day." I nodded.

Being the regent's son, other merrow had to follow certain protocols. Mermaids were to issue me a good day first and then I could choose whether to respond. Mermen needed to wait for *my* good day, at which time they were rule-bound to wish me a good day. However, if I *did not* wish a good day to them, mermen needed to remain silent until addressed.

It might sound complicated, but these were the kind of rules that made life much simpler. Especially in the mornings, when I felt shy or more recently, when my chest hurt worse than normal.

That's why I got upset when ahead of me I noticed a cluster of mermaids. That was against the rules. Main corridors were meant to keep an orderly flow of merrow coming and going, not idle chit-chat.

When they saw me, they broke from their cluster.

"Good day," they said in unison. Then they burst into barely suppressed laughter. Even Seawynn, Ariella's closest friend, had a bemused smile plastered to her face. What had Chrysalis told them?

My face reddened. How dare they laugh at me? I should report them to Krenil for loitering and disorderly conduct.

I knew that I wouldn't though. Ariella had been with them, and I didn't want her to get in trouble. If it were a choice between rules and my sister, she'd win every time.

Ariella hung back and broke away from the mermaids, shooting an angry look. She grabbed my hand. "Ignore them."

"What were they saying?"

"It doesn't matter." She shot me a worried glance. "Maybe we'd better find Krenil. He said he could help?"

For Ariella to recommend Krenil's help, the gossip must have been brutal. We continued toward the Great Auditorium.

Krenil swam with a merman my age—his name was Crusock. Crusock showed off his trident skills near the entrance. Krenil nodded his approval at the young merman's form as he tried a fancy new move. Crusock tossed his weapon in the air, caught it behind his back, then parried forward. When my classmate spotted me, he stopped and a nasty grin spread across his broad, dumb face.

Crusock was Barron's little brother. They could not have been less alike and had despised each other.

"Good day, Krenil," I said. I glared at my classmate and remained silent. He glowered at me, unable to speak to me until I spoke to him.

"Good day, young master, Ariella" Krenil gave a slight tilt of his head.

"Good day, Krenil. We need to talk to you," Ariella said.

Krenil gave Ariella an even deeper bow. "Of course." He turned to Crusock. "Fine work, my boy. Keep it up."

Crusock smirked and smashed into my shoulder as he swam past. "Nice trident, Smelphin," he muttered.

My mouth hung open in shock. He'd spoken to me before I wished him a good day! And made fun of my name?

I glanced at Krenil to see if he'd heard but he was too busy fawning over Ariella. This was all because of what happened with Chrysalis. Well, not all because of her. Crusock had been an ass toward me since we were young fry, but I'm sure he'd never have had the nerve to do something that disrespectful. Until now.

"Brother." Ariella grabbed my hand. "Krenil has a solution to your dilemma."

"Indeed, I do, young master." He spoke to me, but his eyes ravished Ariella, glowing with a feverish desire that made me uncomfortable.

"Well," I said, "what do I do?"

"Prove yourself as a warrior and you may forgo the spawning ritual." He folded his hands in front of his belly.

"Prove myself as a *warrior*?" If it hadn't been such a horrifying idea, I might have laughed. I turned to Ariella. She returned a weak smile. Tango swam to the wall and scratched himself. "Tango! Stop it!" I called.

"Announce your intent to compete in the next tournament without delay." Krenil clapped his hand on my shoulder.

"People die at that tournament! I'm sure Crusock would love to make certain that happens."

Krenil scratched his whiskers. His knife hung glittering at his belt, peeking through the thick seagrass he'd wound around it.

"I know! I'll make you a pouch of spiced coral," Ariella said. "You can toss it in Crusock's face and blind him."

"Cheat?" I said. "Father would exile me—or do what he did to Barron."

"He'd never—"

Krenil nodded. "Spiced coral. Very much against the rules, I'm afraid." He didn't appear to be paying attention. His eyes wandered up and down Ariella's body, while a dreamy look played across his face.

"Krenil, you must help Delphin! Now, I must… speak to Seawynn." Ariella escaped to her friend. Krenil's face darkened.

Abandoned. Even by my sister.

"Krenil? Krenil?" I shook him to get his attention.

"Young Master, the next tournament hasn't been announced. You still have time to prepare. I will help you. I promise."

A horn sounded and young mermen filed into the room along with spectators.

"Announce your intent today, and I'll make certain you have all the support you need to prove yourself."

As I swam in with the others, I watched Krenil swim to Ariella. I'm not sure what he said, but her hand shot out and smacked him hard on the side of the face.

Krenil's face went white, lips pinched. There was a collective murmur as heads turned in their direction. Krenil was second only to my father in command. Though he no doubt had it coming, I worried my sister's action would have consequences. A deep wave of foreboding surged through my stomach.

* * *

We didn't call it the Grand Auditorium for nothing. A giant sphere of white. It was like swimming in an alabaster bubble. The only thing that marred its perfection were several bloodstained areas that had not yet been resurfaced with the special mix we used to plaster over the ancient crystal that lay beneath.

"Control the uncontrollable! Harness raw emotion! Delphin, what's your problem? You're getting worse instead of better," Finner shouted.

Deep scars ran down his right arm and his face was gaunt, bony, and fearsome with a big, bushy black beard. Next to Father, Finner was one of our strongest fighters. His assistant, Kelvin, tossed balls into the center, one after the other. I tried to spear as many as I could before they hit the floor. I hit almost all of them, but only three out of twenty deflated.

"Delphin, what is it? You look ill."

I steeled my mind, ready to announce my intent… but I stopped myself. How could I, after proving myself such a poor student? There was no way Krenil could help.

"Such a pretty trident. A shame he doesn't know how to use it," Crusock said to his friend Ganny loud enough for everyone to hear. Ganny heehawed with laughter, jagged sharp teeth glimmering.

"Crusock! Save it for the ring," Finner warned.

I twirled the trident between my fingers. Krenil gave me my trident as a gift on my last name day. Tridents were sacred. Once you claimed a trident, it wasn't used by anyone else according to our rules.

More handsome than any other trident I'd seen, veins of color mixed with silver and platinum. It was larger than a regular weapon, which made it unwieldy. Krenil told me I'd grow into it. Not so far. I might as well have something beautiful to look at while I embarrassed myself.

Chrysalis waved and blew kisses from the sideline. Surrounded by a cluster of friends, she lifted a kelp frond and allowed it to droop downward. They all burst into laughter. From what I'd gathered, the rumor was that my man parts didn't work right. Impotent was the word they used.

In a weird way, I felt relieved. Father wouldn't execute me for being broken. Would he? There was no need to announce my intent to compete.

"Now, formation!" Kelvin shouted. After target practice, we fell into battle rows and, tridents held forward, swam multiple loops and laps. Here was one area in which I excelled. I was fast. Faster than any of them. Even that didn't help me today.

"In formation, Delphin!" Finner shouted. "This is not a race! You are working as a team! A team!"

I fell back.

"Lunge!" We jabbed our tridents forward.

"Parry!" We stopped dead in the water and jib-jabbed up and then down.

"Sunward!" We swam up at top speed. "Sunburst!" We thrust our tridents toward the top of the sphere. Aim was not that critical. Force was. This movement was the most important skill to perfect for The Hunt.

"A special treat today! Our regent himself will come watch the fruits of your hard-won labor." Finner looked over at me.

Father is coming?

"We'll spend extra time on transmission."

Perfect. My weakest skill. The transmission arts were complex. To transmit one's mind force into a trident turned it from a sharp object to a powerful and deadly weapon. There was the singing side to it and then there was the part that used mindforce. This was the true art that separated a merrow warrior from someone like me. I just flailed a pointy object around.

"Select your opponents!"

Crusock grinned at me. I turned to Aelph, one of the weaker fighters, but it was too late. My nemesis had marked me as his own.

We sparred.

"Yield!" I yelped as he jabbed his silver trident into my chest, drawing a few drops of blood. Today he was even nastier than usual.

"Yield!" I said again. He jabbed harder.

His trident shimmered with energy as he charged it with mindforce. I directed my attention into my trident—it wasn't anger or even fear— it was pure desperation.

C'mon! C'mon! What I needed was to calm my mind and then project.

I thought I detected a slight charge, a slight waver around the weapon. Maybe I was making progress?

My trident grew warm in my hands. Then hot. Otherwise, it didn't change. It appeared there was some aspect of training that I'd missed. All the other mermen—even younger ones—had made better progress. Crusock breached my defense again and nearly slashed my stomach open.

A murmur traveled through the water. Out of the corner of my eye, I saw Father enter the arena. He swam around us in rapid circles, muscular arms tensed as he gripped his trident, single good eye watching me, judging.

His blind eye was covered with a shiny black shell held in place with sea-silk. Good thing he was half-blind. At times like this, it felt as if just his angry look alone might stop my heart. Two eyes might be the end of me.

My trident remained hot in my hand. I glanced at Crusock and noticed him eye my father. He lunged forward and smashed my arm with his shoulder. My trident flew from my hand, spun and hit the bottom of the sphere with a dull *thunk*. He then forced me down at the tip of his weapon. I lay, staining the white surface with my blood, chest heaving.

"Yield!" I shouted.

This time, Crusock obeyed. Father swam up behind him. "Nice work, Crusock." Father clapped his shoulder. "However, a lost trident doesn't warrant a yield. It warrants death. At least in a match. Go spar with someone worth your time."

He waited until Crusock left and then turned his blank baleful eye in my direction.

"How can it be that *you're* my son?" His face wrinkled with disgust as he turned to leave.

Anger and humiliation scalded the back of my throat. I grabbed my trident and righted myself in the water.

"Master Finner!" I shouted. Finner stopped his tutoring and glanced over at me, confused. "I announce my intent to compete in the next tournament!"

Father paused at the doorway. He turned and a flash of surprise crossed his face. He shot me a grim, unreadable look, and nodded.

Chapter Six - Elias

THREE DAYS LATER, Elias' family lay huddled under a tarp in a truck ready to depart for the Adriatic Sea. The Toyota 4x4 truck Timu arranged arrived with room to take all of them, including his father. That's not how it worked out.

Oren ranted on and on about not wanting to leave with them. He made a big show of his leg, how much it pained him. How he wished he could stay and fight for the cause.

Finally, Islar, one of Timu's soldiers, took him at his word.

"Stay then, Oren. We'll find a place for you," Islar said. "If you believe in the cause…"

Oren hesitated for an instant. "Of course, I do!" He stood in front of Inas, Nijah, and a few others. Bluff called. Fear flitted across his face, but it was too late.

"Good." Islar nodded. "You stay then." Islar raised his fist into the air. "For love of the motherland!"

Oren pumped his arm in the air, his tricep, long turned to flab, jiggled beneath his grimy blue shirt. "For love of the motherland!" he repeated, but it sounded hollow.

Inas fell to her knees, tears staining her cheeks. "No, Papa! You're too old! What about your leg? Come with us!"

Elias' eyes stayed dry. Hadn't Father gotten what he'd asked for all this time? There was no reason for tears.

Just before they left, Oren leaned into the rear of the truck. He shoved great-grandfather's sheath into Elias' sweaty hands. "Take this," he said. "It's yours now." As a young boy, Oren forbade him to even touch the sacred object.

Elias took the sheath and looked at his father, eyes wide.
Father knows he will die.

The truck jerked into gear and they headed toward the sea. Elias peered from beneath the tarp and watched through eyes still swollen from his beating. Oren had already disappeared in a billowing plume of beige dust. Elias wiped a tear from his bruised cheek with one angry swipe of his grimy hand.

Chapter Seven - Delphin

IT BECAME A strange comfort knowing I'd likely die soon in the tournament. A relief. After what happened to Barron, I deserved it. However, loose frond-ends remained. For one, tending to Tango's miserable skin condition and making sure he'd be okay without me. I took Tango to Abalon.

Three moonstones in the ceiling emanated dim light in Abalon's healing chamber. Her healing beds were empty. It had been several moons since the last Hunt and most other day-to-day injuries were minor.

I waited for her to give medicine to an older mermaid who had sprained her fin while plastering one of the western corridors. I couldn't remember the woman's name but her face reddened when she saw me.

"Good day." She lowered her eyes.

"Good day," I responded.

She swam from the chamber giving a flitting glance behind her as she left.

"No dolphins in the healing ward!" Abalon waved her hand to shoo Tango away. He darted toward the ceiling, a hurt look in his eyes and swam in a slow, lazy circle.

"Were you hurt during trident practice?" Abalon swam to me, inspecting my torso.

"Just a scratch. No, it's Tango." I coaxed him down, pointing to the sores on his flank.

Abalon reached out and touched one of his wounds. "He has the flake. It won't kill him. It's not contagious to us." She gave me a blank stare.

"Well, that's good but gosh, he's so miserable. Do you have

something you could give him?"

"Young master, we have a tournament coming and then our next Hunt soon after. There *will* be injuries… and deaths." Her face darkened.

I swallowed.

"I cannot spare a single gram of my salves for… your pet. In time, the beast will heal on its own. And if it doesn't? Well, I suppose being the regent's son has its perks, but keeping a pet such as this is not wise. Let him go."

My eyes flashed. "Let him go? I'm *not* keeping him here. Tango wants to stay with me. He's an orphan, remember? He'd be dead if not for me."

"Perhaps you might offer it to our post Hunt feast? That would end its misery. It looks like it still has a few tender nibbles left on its flanks." She bared her teeth.

I swam in front of Tango, blocking him from view. "Offer him up for dinner? Never! He could leave anytime he liked! But he won't. He is afraid of the open sea. I rescued him and I won't let anyone hurt him!" I shouted.

Abalon drew back, hand to her breast. Unlike my father, I was not one to raise my voice. I prided myself on that. Now, none of that seemed to matter. Pride. Or fearing that I might offend someone or hurt his or her feelings. Not when it came to protecting Tango.

"C'mon, Tango." I raced from her chamber. Tango followed. A pang of fear tore through my heart. Who would ever care as much for Tango as I did, if I were gone?

* * *

I found Krenil supervising work in the western section in the Hall of Order. There was plenty of work to be done. Every day, merrow continued to plaster, replacing the old with the new.

During the final stage, soldiers came and sung into their tridents. This created a vibration that hardened the material to the walls. This was another task I'd failed at. I couldn't achieve sufficient vibration through my weapon.

It wasn't suitable work for the regent's son. Although if I'd proven my skill, I might have taken some burden off Krenil as a supervisor.

He did so much for me; I hated to ask for another favor. Plus, I'd promised to put in a good word for him with Ariella. The last time I'd seen them together, she'd slapped him across the face.

"Let's swim off on our own." Krenil's eyes twinkled in light from the moonstones.

I explained my fears for Tango once I died.

"Badly wounded, possible. But die? What makes you think you'll die in the tournament?" Krenil asked.

"It happens. I've seen it happen to those better than me. What makes you think I'll live?"

"Young master, I promised I'd help you. When have I ever neglected my promises to you?"

I swallowed guilt and a measure of gratitude. "Never."

"Follow me. I might as well give it to you now."

Krenil led me toward his extensive chambers. We swam past the cell where, Alec, our next sacrificial merrow, was being held. It was filled with fine foods and more luxurious than even Father's chambers.

Most sacrifices were honored to serve—or at least they pretended to be. It's not like they had any choice. Not Alec. He lunged at me through the bars, teeth bared. Krenil hurried by my side, smacking his trident against the bars with a clang that made my teeth ache. "Back, you ungrateful blubber!"

Alec snarled. "Ungrateful? Come in here and I'll show you gratitude. You did this to me, Krenil! I know you're somehow responsible!"

Krenil shook his head and pulled me along into the maze of white passages that led to his quarters. "Wait here."

I floated in the anteroom. A comfortable sea-silk lounger sat beneath pristine, white walls. When Krenil returned, he held a shiny, silver trident in his hands.

"I'll loan you this one for the tournament." He smiled.

"But what about *my* trident?" Krenil had given it to me. I'd grown attached to it. I liked my trident even if it caused me some trouble. Different from everyone else's, it was the envy of other mermen my age.

"It was a mistake to give you such an advanced weapon," he said. "This one is just what you need."

"Whose trident was this?" I ran my fingers along the smooth metal of the weapon.

"Barron's."

My chest flashed with pain and bile rose in my throat. I took deep breaths of water, cloaking as hard I could and trying not to throw-up.

"Barron's? I can't," I said. "It wouldn't be right." I held it out to him.

"Why not?" Krenil said, head cocked the side. "He's dead. You deserve it far more than him. He wasn't worthy of our pod. You are, young master." He looked me in the eye and cocked his head to the right. "You know that, don't you?"

I didn't answer. "His trident will be better?"

Krenil forced it back toward me. "Try it."

I took a few practice swipes. It was smaller and lighter than mine.

Krenil folded his arms and swam a few paces back, observing. "Careful now. It's an older trident. You may have to put more force into it than you're accustomed to. But it's nimble. It should serve its purpose. You need not fear dying. My advice is that you don't use this trident until the tournament though. No reason to allow Crusock to plan." Krenil winked.

I nodded. Placing the trident against the white wall, I wrapped Krenil in a spontaneous hug. "Thank you."

"Now, now, no need for that." Krenil broke away. "There is something you can do for me. It's about Ariella."

I braced myself for another request I wouldn't be able to fulfill. Why couldn't he have fallen for some other mermaid?

"Talk to her, will you? I feel we've got off on quite the wrong foot. What can I do to please her? To win her affection? You must find out and tell me. The Regent supports my claim. She might as well stop fighting the inevitable. During the next spawning ceremony, she will be of age. I want this to be a cause of celebration for us both."

Chapter Eight - Elias

ELIAS, INAS, AND Nijah spent the day crammed into the back of the dusty 4x4. True to his promise, Timu's man got them to the shore. Coughing out the last remains of road dirt, Elias stood rubbing his eyes in a chaotic seaside port. A small fishing village turned refuge.

Hundreds of other families who looked as lost and desperate as them arrived with suitcases, backpacks, and makeshift wagons that carried treasured belongings.

"Where now?" Inas asked the driver as he folded up the tarp and tossed it in the back, eager to return home. "Is there a boat?" She eyed the crowd.

"I've done my part," he snapped as he leaped into his truck and slammed the door. "The rest is up to you."

It was chaotic with the fighting back home, but here, in some ways, it was worse. So many people!

Three men herded refugees one after the other into a fishing boat that sunk lower and lower in the water. It seemed impossible but they fit five more. The boat's captain started a belching motor. Out of all the passengers, the tiny boat's captain was the only one who wore a tattered life jacket.

Elias hadn't seen the sea in years. Not since he'd helped his uncle one summer. He'd since died in the fighting.

Exhaust, sweat, and desperation mixed with the deeper smells of the ocean. A salty tang stung his nostrils. Humidity left his back drenched in sweat. At home, the desert wicked away moisture faster than it could gather. Aside from a bit of dampness beneath his armpits, Elias wasn't used to sweating like this.

They weren't yet out on the water, but already Elias felt as if he swam. Although he barely knew how. Neither did his mom or sister.

He spoke to several other families and learned that the tiny boat they'd watched depart would cost them all their money and more. If Inas sold her wedding ring, there would be enough for the three of them.

"To go on a little boat like that in the ocean? For what?" Nijah asked. "To drown?"

"Better than being shot!" Inas said. She looked hot and tired. "At least there's a chance for a new life."

Elias hoped this was true. A few seconds later, his heart lifted at the sight of a large ship coming into port. They clustered around the boat. Most others kept a healthy distance. Men with machine guns appeared on deck and fired bullets into the water. People scattered.

The ship docked and a group of men marched out a woman and a man, blindfolded. Then came crates of what appeared to be electronics. A flat-screen TV and other items.

"Pirates." An older man leaned toward Inas as he whispered and spat on the ground. She grabbed Nijah's hand.

"We should go back home!" Nijah's eyes grew wide with fear.

"Home?" Inas grabbed her arm. "There is no home! Look! Look around you. You think these people are here for vacation? They're running from the same things we are. We have no choice."

Later that afternoon, they handed over the last of their money and Inas' ring to a young guy with a diamond stud pierced through his nose.

The gray fishing boat was only moderately better than the last boat Elias had seen. That would have been promising, but if not for the fact that an even greater number of people were packed inside. Soon the boat sunk close to the waterline. They were the last to board.

There were two barrels of water on the floor of the boat. No food.

"How long is the trip?" Nijah asked.

"Two days," a rheumy-eyed woman answered. Inas began to pray under her breath.

"If there's a good current," a bearded man with dark rings beneath his eyes answered, not bothering to look up.

Elias took his sister's hand and held it until Nijah calmed. He felt an enormous weight of responsibility descend. If not for Timu's help, they wouldn't be here.

"It's good if the boat sinks. If boat sinks, the Europeans... they come rescue," one old man said with a wink.

Hot sun scorched Elias' neck as their boat chugged into the open water, belching sour diesel from its engine.

Meanwhile, more and more people arrived at the dock since they boarded. The population of the small town had at least tripled in the one day they'd arrived.

"This is the right choice." Inas grabbed Elias' chin in her hand and forced him to look at her. "The only choice."

"One day, you'll have a story to tell, that's for sure," the old man said.

"A story to tell our grandkids, huh, Nijah?" Elias leaned against his sister. They smiled at each other for the first time in what felt like days. Nijah's eyes sparkled like the water. For a moment, it felt as if they were at the start of an adventure. A honking, snort of laughter interrupted the moment.

"If you *live* to have grandkids!" the rheumy old woman added with a horrible, raspy cough.

Chapter Nine - Delphin

AFTER MY VISIT with Krenil, I snuck to my chambers through the hidden back corridors and stashed my new trident. I didn't want to give Crusock any opportunity to strategize against me.

Tango swam next to me as I set off to find Ariella. I dreaded relaying the conversation I'd had with Krenil. Perhaps I wouldn't die after all? And if one problem got solved, weren't all problems solvable? Even Ariella's.

Krenil was an honorable man and a dear friend. Okay, not the most attractive merman and old, but there was no merrow aside from Father who held a higher rank. If I were in Ariella's position, I'd be no more enthused than she was. For Krenil's sake, I hoped Ariella wasn't the only mermaid he had his eye on.

Tango scratched his flank along the wall.

"Stop it! You're making it worse. Poor fellow. I'll figure out something else to help you, I promise."

The corridors changed their appearance. No longer smoothed pristine white and patched over with the plaster we'd created. Now they were dark, mottled crystal covered in algae. Some living crystal still flickered with light. Most areas lay dark and in shadow. I'd entered a forbidden area. I didn't dare illuminate my arc crystal until I was well inside.

This will be the last time I break the rules.

After they executed Barron, they'd left his body buried where it lay, crushed.

I remembered Father's words. *"He's not worthy to lie with decent merrow."*

I swam past pillars, pieces of shattered crystal, and other detritus that lay near the gates to the old palace. Soon, I arrived at the site of his execution.

"From decadence he rose and to decadence he will return. A symbol of all that led us to ruin," Father had announced after the giant slab of stone crushed the life from Barron's strong, healthy body.

I'd been too upset to notice but now I saw that several pieces of statue were too large to break. Some remained intact. The hand of one rested on another's back. His giant stone head had tilted toward the other, full lips open to meet his mate. These statues had once shown two mermen in an embrace. Now Barron's bones lay broken beneath.

I touched Barron's trident to the top of the pile and closed my eyes.

"Thank you, Barron," I said. My body shook.

Several years older than me, Barron had been the son my father wished he'd had. Deft with his trident and a strong fighter. Where I was thin and lean, Barron was buff and full of muscle. Yet he was smart too with a whimsical sense of humor and a smile that made his hazel eyes sparkle.

Barron was Crusock's older brother. Their parents were killed during the Great War. Common to many fry, they'd been raised by the pod. Barron and Crusock's rivalry was legendary.

As Crusock grew older, his love of fighting became legendary. Crusock fought well, better than most, but Barron remained several notches above. To add to Crusock's resentment, Barron refused to teach his younger brother after Crusock attacked and seriously wounded a fellow student over some minor disagreement.

Meanwhile, Barron took me under his wing. Before Krenil became such a large part of my life, it was Barron I turned to as a mentor. That was… until I killed him.

No one knew this. No one ever would.

I draped myself over the large stone merman and my chest heaved.

"I'm sorry, Barron. I'm so, so sorry for what I did."

* * *

Afterward, I swam to the abandoned palace Ariella had found. Here, the walls weren't bare and white. They were made of blackened crystal that had glowed and shone once upon a time.

I hurried through a garden grotto where hundreds of plants grew. Soon I found the place. A small bed of glowing, iridescent story shells. I dug among them and found Ariella's favorite.

I put it to my ear and listened. It told the story of a mermaid who traveled to the surface and fell in love with a human boy. He grew a fin and returned to the sea with her, where they lived happily ever after.

Would I ever love someone like that? Ha! Doubtful. My heart felt as brittle and hardened as the plaster in Krenil's Hall of Order.

Chapter Ten - Delphin

"DELPHIN!"

Tingles ran up my spine. I whirled around, trident raised. Then I relaxed. It was Ariella.

"Interesting. You said you wouldn't come here again." She folded her arms, a half-smile on her face. "That didn't last long. Couldn't resist the story shells?"

"Not exactly. I-I had to come. Krenil lent Barron's trident to me. I came to pay my respects and thought I'd find you on the way." I gave her a sheepish grin. "You know, Krenil really wants to help. He's not a bad guy."

Ariella rolled her eyes. "He's a lecherous fool, and he'll never have me."

Maybe now wasn't the time to tell her about Father agreeing to their match? Tango scratched himself against the mottled crystal wall.

"What's wrong with Tango?" Ariella swam to him.

"He has the Flake. He's miserable. "

"Ask Abalon for some herbs."

"Already did. No luck. Do you know of an herb that might help?"

Ariella stroked Tango's flank. "Hmmm."

"What *hmm*?"

"I don't know of an herb. But I know someone who might."

"Really, who?" Tango swam over and nudged me under my armpit. "Quit it, Tango! That tickles." Tango returned to scratching against the rocks. "He's so itchy."

"Let me borrow Tango," she said. "I'll bring him right back."

"He won't leave my side ever since he got sick," I said. "It's like he thinks I'm his mom. I'll go with you."

"No." Ariella wouldn't meet my eyes.

"Why not?"

"This person... doesn't want their presence known...." Ariella trailed off.

"Do you think I'm incapable of keeping a secret?" I scrunched my fists tight. "I'm better now!"

"You are getting better at cloaking," she admitted.

"I *can* keep secrets, Ariella. I promise."

Ariella nodded. "He mentioned wanting to see you at some point. Maybe now will be fine. Let's go."

"He wants to see me? Who?" Now I burned with curiosity. Ariella didn't answer.

We wound deeper and deeper into the forbidden areas. Far past the garden of story shells. Farther than I'd ever gone. The passages wound and circled in endless loops.

"How large did our pod used to be?" I marveled at the height of the large cavernous room we entered. Row upon row of circular objects were inlaid in glowing crystal walls that extended up into darkness.

"Our pod used to be enormous. Thousands? Hundreds of thousands?" Ariella let out a soft but piercing whistle. "Our secret code," she explained. "He'll be here soon."

"What are those things?" I pointed at the circular receptacles in the crystal.

"Scrolls!" she said. "This was the old palace library. I found it the other day. Amazing, isn't it? The crystal still lives here." She spread her arms.

"You've been reading stories without me?"

She shook her head. "Better than story shells. Scrolls hold ancient knowledge. I'm learning about the past. And our future. Father is wrong."

"About what?"

"The Tentacle God. He won't save us. He'll destroy us. It's more important than ever that we take action. There's a prophecy about two girls. The Atlantis Twins. There are several scrolls missing. Uncle thinks they were taken to the human world."

"To the human world? Why?"

Ariella swam up to a scroll, took it out, and examined it, face scrunched with concentration. "Precious knowledge is valued everywhere I'd imagine. At least by those wise enough to recognize it."

"Do you still hope to fall in love with a human one day?" I teased.

She sighed. "I'm afraid that only happens in story shells. Plus, that's very much against the rules, as you know."

I snorted bubbles through my nose. "Since when have you cared about rules?"

Tango nosed around at the bottom, looking for food. My anticipation grew with each minute. "Well, is this person coming or not?"

"He's probably scavenging in the swirl. He collects human objects."

"What's the swirl?"

"C'mon. Let's go."

We swam through a series of passages that became increasingly narrow.

A cool current sent my hair billowing behind me and I detected a new scent. "This leads to open water!" I'd never visited the open sea. The closest I'd gotten was our sea gates.

"Farther still." She darted ahead.

We weren't allowed to swim into the open sea. Only during our hunts. Another rule soon to be broken. I should keep an official count. My list of crimes, broken rules, and misdeeds was becoming impressive.

We emerged through a narrow gap and entered a ring of coral. My mouth dropped open. He had his head down as he sifted through sand in a circular patch of sand surrounded by coral. His face broke into a smile when he saw Ariella. When he noticed me, the smile faded. Uncle Nebulon raced across to us.

"Uncle, I thought you were dead—" I started but didn't have time to finish my thought before he pinned me against a wall of coral. My trident fell from my grip and stuck in the sandy loam.

"You!" he said. Anger poured off him in waves. "Ariella, you should know better than to bring him here!"

"I thought you wanted to see him!" Ariella put her hand to her heart.

"I did. But on my terms. It's too dangerous to have him here."

Without warning, Uncle Nebulon reached out his will and probed my mind, hard. I tried to cloak, but he was already inside. I threw up a shield, but it was too late. He plundered my deepest fears and desires. It felt like rape.

"Stop!" I screamed. "What's your problem?"

"Make me stop!" Uncle Nebulon shouted. "Grow up, boy!"

I felt as if I were going insane. "Please," I moaned.

"Uncle, don't hurt him!" Ariella pulled at his arm.

He ignored her. His eyes burned into me, furious.

Somehow, I wrested back control. Forcing my heart to still, I let my mind sink into my body. *An empty mind is a cloaked mind. A thing no longer there cannot be seen.* He probed harder and caught onto… nothing. His mental grip slipped.

I allowed my thoughts to return and felt him catch onto one. But it was a fake-out. The moment he grabbed hold, I cut the thought loose and dropped my mind back into my body. His grip failed, sending him tumbling from my mind space. He made a second attempt. I threw up a shield and grasped *his mind* the moment he tried. Caught off guard, for a flash I caught a scrap of thought… a wound.

Barron.

It was Uncle Nebulon who I'd seen kissing Barron! I glimpsed the pain, sadness, and loss he felt. With his chiseled features and warrior body, Uncle Nebulon was an attractive merman. However, I'd never considered him in that way before. He was much older than Barron. I was the more obvious match. Guilt and envy surged through me.

A look of fury crossed Nebulon's face, and he kicked me out of his mind so hard that my teeth ached. His jaw quivered with anger. He raised his trident.

"Uncle! What are you doing?" Ariella grabbed at his arm.

His eyes cleared. A tear bubble popped from his eye and floated away. He appeared shaken. Tipping his head toward me, he said, "Nice work, Delphin. You cloaked well."

Dazed, I nodded. My chest hurt worse than it had in days. My mouth felt like it was stuffed with kelpfloss.

When I'd recovered enough to collect my thoughts, I turned to my uncle. He hung in front of me, head bowed, lost in his own private grief.

"Uncle, I loved Barron like a brother—" I blushed, remembering that I loved him a bit differently than a brother but pushed that thought aside. "I wish that I could—."

"Ah, you're just a naïve boy. It's not you I blame."

"Blame for what?" Ariella turned from me to my uncle. I braced myself and waited for Uncle Nebulon to tell her. Did he know what had happened?

I'd told no one what happened between Barron and me. Not even Ariella. Part of me wanted him to tell her. Instead, Uncle Nebulon went silent, staring at me hard until I looked away.

Then he spotted my trident. He grabbed it, eyes wide.

"This is Barron's! Where did you get it?"

"Krenil."

Uncle Nebulon spat to the side. "I might have known. Well, it's a fine weapon. A very fine weapon. Krenil must have a great deal of respect for you." He paused before he handed it to me.

"Are you okay with me using it? I can try to get it back to you—after the tournament, I mean." I regretted the offer. Krenil wanted it returned.

Uncle Nebulon waved his hand. "Bah. I'm not sentimental about objects. Wield it in good health, nephew. I hope it serves you better than it did poor Barron."

Tango nudged me with his nose.

"You still have your dolphin, I see? They haven't convinced you to eat him?" Uncle Nebulon gave Tango a gentle pat on his flank.

"No!" I put my arm around Tango and stroked his dorsal fin—it felt as silky and smooth as a pearl. "Poor guy has the Flake."

Ariella swam forward. "Uncle, I thought you could—"

She didn't even need to ask. "I haven't survived this long alone without learning all the places that the healing plants grow. Wait here."

Nebulon left to find materials to heal Tango's ailment.

"Delphin, what—?"

I interrupted her before she could start asking questions. "All this time, I thought Uncle Nebulon died during the Great War! How long have you been visiting?"

"Not long after you showed me the secret entry."

I picked up a strange, circular object. The area was littered with many bones but also unfamiliar objects.

"Human treasures," Ariella explained. "The current carries them here and they get trapped in the coral formation. Uncle Nebulon thinks they may be useful."

I lifted my fingers and felt the current rush between them. Lighter objects—scraps of wood, small pieces of shell, and colorful bits and bobs of human trash—were pulled through to the other side. There they got sucked deeper down into the blackest parts of the sea. Heavier items became trapped in the grotto.

"Yesterday we found a human leg!" Ariella said. "But it wasn't a real leg. Uncle has it."

"What do you mean a human leg?"

"Humans can live without legs, it seems. Sometimes, they make fake ones."

I thrust my fin against the current and hovered over an array of fascinating debris. I picked up a circular object with orange and red cartoon shells painted on its surface.

"What is this?"

"Plastic," Ariella said, nose wrinkled. "It's killing the ocean."

Plastic. I tested the word in my mind. There was a lot of it in all different colors and configurations. A bright shiny object lying right on top of the sand caught my attention. Made of metal, a cracked layer of glass protected a salt-damaged image in the center.

Three humans stood smiling. Two of the figures were hard to see. However, the third to the left I could make out. A human male in his teens, about the same age as me, at least in merrow years. I wondered if human years were the same?

Sparkling brown eyes and brilliant, square, white teeth made his full, red lips stand out even more. He stood on dry land. No water anywhere. Nothing but browns and beiges with a patch of blue sky visible at the top.

My heart fluttered at this direct glimpse of life on the surface. The surface! It looked as magical as it sounded in the story shell. Perhaps I would go there one day, after all? Now I could see how it held appeal to Ariella.

Beside it lay an ornate sheath that was missing its knife. I picked it up. Just as I did, bells rang far in the distance.

I turned to Ariella, eyes wide. Without moonstones to guide us, we'd lost track of the time.

"The choosing!" we said in unison.

Chapter Eleven - Delphin

"Where's Uncle? We need to get back." Crystal bells continued to chime far in the distance.

"Let me see that." Ariella took the sheath from me.

My eyes returned to the photo. It wasn't a story shell and yet I felt the same sensation of being drawn into something bigger than the merrow world. Something wonderful. The boy was so handsome, his eyes held a mysterious light as if on the verge of asking an essential question.

"This is Lemurian magic." Ariella held up the sheath.

"I thought I might keep it and the photo."

Ariella frowned. "Why?"

"The sheath is like nothing I've ever seen and yet somehow familiar. And the photo holds a story. I want to learn how to listen to it."

"Keep the photo, fine. But not that thing."

"Is it dangerous?"

"The Lemurians are all dead, but…"

Long ago, the Lemurians were our enemies. Ariella turned the sheath over in her hands.

"What does it say?"

"I can't read it. Without the blade, I suppose it can't do any harm." She handed it back.

When Nebulon returned, he carried a small urn in his hands. "Put this on your dolphin twice each day. This will clear the Flake."

* * *

We returned to the boring, white tunnels of our pod. Bells continued to ring.

"Maybe I'll be the next sacrifice," I joked. "At this rate, it might be for the best."

Ariella slapped me. "Don't say that! Things will improve. Krenil gave you your new trident."

"Yes, but since when did you have any confidence in Krenil?"

"For a start, he looks at me with different eyes than you."

"Thank goodness!" I laughed.

Ariella snickered. "Look, we were once a people of laughter and celebration. All these rules and regulations he creates with Father—it can't last. It's not the truth of who we are." She kissed me on the forehead before we split off and went separate ways.

I stuck to the back routes, wanting to be certain no one spotted me with my trident... or the photo. I'd left the sheath hidden back in the forbidden area but I couldn't bear to leave the photo behind. I wanted to study it more.

After I stashed my trident and the photo in my quarters, I swam with hundreds of other merrow headed in the same direction.

A few merrow wore frightened looks while others grinned with excitement. Crusock fell into the latter camp. He spotted me from across the passage. He waved and kissed his bicep, then pretended to wield a trident and stab it forward. Tridents were forbidden in the Hall of Tentacles. A palm touched my shoulder and I jumped.

"Young Master." Krenil looked pale. Dark circles lingered beneath his eyes. "Did you speak with Ariella? I haven't been able to find her."

I swallowed and nodded. "Maybe I should tell you her answer in private?"

"I see." Krenil's face darkened further. "I expected as much. She's too willful for her own good. You aren't to blame. Thank you for trying."

They held the sacrifices in the Hall of Tentacles. Unlike the other mundane rooms, each one the same, this one was fascinating, although it terrified me. Similar to most rooms, it was a white orb. That all changed at the ceiling.

Several tentacles poked from a hole in the top center. Each day, specially chosen assistants chipped away, making it bigger. The bigger it got, the more tentacles that emerged. How large would get?

Each tentacle was covered in multiple eyes that roved about the giant space. It felt as though they all looked at me, though I was certain it was my imagination. Krenil told me they were eyes that could not see.

Two of Father's guards dragged Alec into the center. He bit, thrashed, and struggled, swearing at the men. It shocked me.

Paying homage to the Tentacle God was meant to protect us from our human oppressors and regenerate the merrow species. To be sacrificed was, well, not quite an honor, it meant leaving our pod. However, it was a duty that most were proud to perform. Not Alec.

He screamed and bit one of the guard's ears. Blood swirled in the clear water. A collective murmur rushed through the crowd of several hundred that had gathered.

The guard raised the butt of his trident and bashed Alec in the side of his head, leaving him semi-conscious.

Krenil swam to Father's right side, Finner and Teomath on the left. They hovered below the tentacles but elevated above the crowd who watched with rapt expressions on their faces.

Krenil handed Father the knife he carried everywhere. Father lifted the blade high in the air. A thrill of recognition ran through me. The knife had the same odd shape as the sheath I'd found!

The thought got brushed from my mind as Father grabbed a tentacle and, with a quick swipe of the knife, cut off a small piece and forced it down Alec's throat.

Alec's eyes opened and fluttered. He coughed and choked, clutching at his throat. In moments, he grew calm. Once he'd stilled, the guards held his arms.

"Alec, go with honor to the upper world. Bring back that what the Tentacle Lord most desires. Help ensure riches and everlasting harmony."

With those words, Father raised Krenil's blade and jammed it down between his fin. Alec shrieked. It raced through my head and felt like it might split me apart. Pain. Anger. Fear.

Alec's fin had split and two legs were growing. A shudder ran through the crowd.

"Send him to The Tentacle Lord!" Father commanded. Finner and Teomath led Alec up to the tentacles and forced him through the opening. The crowd cheered.

The former elation and excitement in the crowd faded when the tip of his foot disappeared. Now came the part I dreaded even more. *The Choosing.*

Only Father and the council members were immune. They were needed to keep the pod functioning. Once they retired, that would change. Currently, even I was fair game.

We put our faith in a greater wisdom. If that meant sacrificing the Regent's son, the pod trusted a purpose greater than our understanding. Regents were as easily made as born, so the saying went. If I got selected, there were plenty of other young mermen eager to take my place.

With the help of Crusock, Krenil dragged out a large white receptacle filled with broken pieces of shell. Selection Shells. We used them for numerous purposes. Lining up one-by-one, we swam past, and each took a half-piece of shell. Mine was brown and white, jagged at the edges.

Shells in hand, we headed toward the sole entrance that led from the room.

Abalon was two merrow in front. Her hand shook as she gave her Selection Shell to the guard. He cupped it in his hand and squinted as he compared it to the one he held. Dropping both in a second white bowl, he waved her on.

My turn soon. Moments later, I held out my white and brown shell. The guard took it, inspected it and looked me in the eye. For a moment, he hesitated. He looked down and compared the shells a second time, then he waved me on. *Phew.* They weren't a match.

Outside in the hall, I leaned against the rough wall and patted Tango while I waited for Ariella. Crowds made him nervous. Not the least because some merrow looked at him with hunger in their eyes. Behind me: a commotion.

"No! This cannot be!" Ariella raced from the Hall of Tentacles. Two guards trailed behind her, stunned looks on their faces.

"Grab her!" the guard said. But Ariella was gone.

Krenil appeared, shaking his head. I swam to him.

"What happened?" I asked.

"Ariella was chosen. She is the next sacrifice."

"What? That's not possible…"

Krenil held up two shells and pieced them together.

"I'm afraid it is," he said with a long sigh. "She has hiding places, so I've heard. Do you know them?"

He reached out and probed but I cloaked and glared at him, offended. "No. I know nothing of them."

My heart thudded in my chest. Poor Ariella was to be sacrificed? Tear bubbles formed at the corners of my eyes.

Chapter Twelve - Delphin

SEVERAL DAYS PASSED and Ariella remained in hiding. If she didn't want to be found, I doubted they ever would. I knew where I could find her if needed, but I didn't dare. Maybe it was my imagination, but Father's guards kept popping up in unexpected places. They had their eyes on me.

I missed her, but I had to stay focused. The tournament was coming up fast. If I ever wanted to see my sister again, it would help to stay alive.

I spent most of my time alone in my room, practicing with the trident Krenil gave me. For several hours, Krenil came and tutored me.

We parried and thrusted working on the energetic bond meant to exist between a merman and his trident. I'd never gotten the hang of that. Now, on the morning of the tournament, I won't say I felt confident. Chances were I'd be injured. But I felt I could put up a passable defense that might save my life.

"Remember what I told you," Krenil said.

I sighed. "I won't drop the trident. I'm certain of that." It felt like it had become part of my body. My hands ached from holding it.

* * *

When I arrived, the Tournament Hall was packed with excited, chattering merrow. As a young fry, tournaments were one of my favorite events. They were exciting diversions—if you weren't the one fighting.

Most merrow spent their days laboring at the extensive patchwork needed to plaster over the old crystal structures. Working with the finicky material was tedious, mindless physical work. This was a pleasant distraction. As I entered with ten other participants, a cheer arose.

We passed a row of guards. One held out a sea-silk pouch. I reached in and grabbed a selection shell. I wasn't certain what the shell was for. We'd already been assigned our fight partners. Unfortunately, mine was Crusock.

"Yoohoo, Delphin! Oh, Delphin!" Chrysalis giggled with two friends as she held up a limp kelp frond. Hadn't I seen this joke before? Good to know that that it hadn't gotten old for her.

I waved and forced a confident smile. The malicious shine in her eyes faded. Meanwhile, my stomach twisted itself into knots so complex I wondered if it would become my life's work to unwind them. Assuming I lived.

As we settled into two rows, Crusock whipped his tail around when he turned. His fin smacked across my chest before I could dodge back.

"Hey!" I grabbed his arm.

He widened his eyes in mock surprise. "Gosh, didn't see you." He flicked my hand off. I was about to say something when the room went quiet. Father entered with Krenil.

Father was an impressive merman, even more so today in his battle garb. My body was like my mother's: lithe, thin, nimble but not muscular. Father was wider than me by three.

He wore a fine, bright red sea-silk tunic cut in such a way that it showed off every battle scar that crisscrossed his impressive body. The way the tunic undulated in the water, it looked like blood flowing above his enormous green-blue fin.

"I have a special announcement!" Father's voice boomed in my head. "In honor of the Hunt tomorrow and at Krenil's suggestion, I will spar the most deserving warrior today."

Excited clicks traveled through the crowd. Father turned to Krenil. I did not want to face Father.

A sudden chill worked his way up my spine. Whatever happened, I needed to make sure I was *not* the most deserving. Inside, I smiled. That shouldn't be difficult.

"I have given each fighter a selection shell to determine the order." More clicks and cheering rose throughout the room. Krenil worked his way down the line and paired fighters together.

To my deep dismay, not only were Crusock and I slotted to face each other, we were the last two mermen on the roster.

Fights flashed past in a blur of limbs, tridents, and occasional swirls of blood. By the time we reached the second-to-last pair, not a single merman had dropped his trident. None had been killed or even injured.

Every year, at least one merman died, sometimes more. It was expected. Dare I say, craved by the crowd. Not by me. Last year, I'd left before anyone got injured. To be honest, my favorite part was watching handsome mermen at the peak of health and vitality grapple with one another.

As Crusock and I swam to the center, the crowd let up a rabid cry.

"Bleed him!" someone shouted. I wasn't sure whether they referred to Crusock or me. I gripped my trident tight and faced the crowd.

For a moment, there was silence. Then Father flung his hand down and let out the whistle that began our match.

Dashing toward me, Crusock went on the offensive. Pushing down hard with my fin, I shot toward the ceiling and looped around. I skimmed above the rowdy merrow audience.

Crusock tried to keep up but saw he was seriously outmatched. Speed was my strongest attribute. I was the fastest merrow in our pod. He returned to the center, flexed his muscles, and taunted me.

"Too afraid to fight? Poor little fry. Here fishy!" He beckoned with his stubby fingers.

Ignoring him, I glanced up at the moonstones. Each tournament lasted a maximum of twenty moonits. Eighteen more left. Although I might not have been a strong fighter like Father, I was a *smart* fighter. Brute physical force was not my forte.

I would use rules instead. Father often said that there was nothing more important. Now, I'd show him that I understood and knew how to strategize. What could be more important for a future leader?

Crusock grew impatient. He launched at me with a burst of speed that caught me off guard. I swooped low then up and around in a wide arcing circle and watched as he exhausted himself again. He fell back, red-faced and furious.

I barely felt winded. I could keep this up for as long as needed. My grasp of the trident was firm. I could swim at top speed with no risk of dropping it. I saw no way for Crusock to harm me. For the first time in the fight, a glow of confidence nestled in my belly.

"Fight me, coward!" he said.

"Can't you see?" I matched his disdain. "I *am* fighting yet you don't seem to notice!" The crowd burst into raucous noises. Many clicked, a few let out raspy buzzes. Mainly though, it seemed I had their grudging approval. Father hovered, watching, arms folded, a bemused look on his face.

Behind me, a scream of laughter distracted me. I turned.

"Oh, Delphin!" Chrysalis dangled the seaweed frond over her mouth while her friends egged her on. As soon as she caught my attention, her razor-sharp teeth snapped over the frond and she tore it off and shook it.

In the split second I got distracted, Crusock was on me. I dodged but not fast enough. His trident pierced my right fin midway down. Searing pain shot through the muscle.

Blood swirled through the water. At the sight of it, the crowd erupted in a mind-numbing cheer. I swam as fast as I could. With my injured fin, it was not fast enough. Crusock circled around and blocked me.

"So what is it I haven't noticed?" He jabbed his trident toward me, taunting. "I notice your blood. Soon there'll be much, much more." I jerked back, missing getting stabbed again.

The sight of my blood made me dizzy. My head ached, teeth chattered. How much blood had I lost? I hazarded a quick peek down at my wound. It wasn't deep. I wouldn't bleed to death.

This calmed me. I focused again. I met Crusock's steely gaze and raised my trident. We circled each other as the crowd went wild. He jabbed and I feinted. He pushed me back farther and farther. Soon I was trapped, backed up against one of the pristine white walls.

Crusock raised his trident and the clicking from the audience reached a feverish pitch.

"Goodbye, Delphin." With a fearsome cry, he plunged his trident toward me with all his force. Out of pure instinct, I rammed my trident upward at the same instant.

It hit his weapon inches from my body. A strange percussive wave shot through my arms. I felt a jolt and saw a blinding light. Next thing I knew, Crusock's' trident twirled high above his head. It spun through the water up toward the cavernous ceiling and landed far away in the center of the arena with a distant, metallic *clunk*. Crusock had lost his trident! For a moment, I could not believe it.

The audience hushed. Then they began to chant. "Blood, blood, blood!"

Crusock looked down at his fallen trident and for many long moments didn't meet my eyes. Lips quivering, he forced his head up. Defeat smoldered in his eyes as he spread his palms and offered his chest to me.

Now rules dictated that he must die. Hands shaking, I lifted my trident, swallowed.

"Well, get it over with, will you, Smelphin?" he whispered low in my head. A private communication just for me.

I moved the trident point to touch his muscular torso. I'd never found Crusock attractive. Unlike his brother, he was too course, too mean. But his physique was impressive. His stomach heaved, rippling with muscle. Pulsing at his neck, his heart beat fast. Now I was supposed to end Crusock's life? Just like that?

The crowd grew impatient. My arms shook as I steadied my trembling hands and readied myself to stab him. Then I glanced at his face again.

He looked very different from Barron and yet, something of his brother lived in his eyes, peering out at me. Especially in this vulnerable moment, when his life was near to ending. Tear bubbles sprang from my eyes, blinding me.

I'd killed poor Barron. It was too late to bring him back. But I couldn't kill Crusock too. I lowered my trident, and a sob wracked my chest.

Confused and angry murmurs swirled through the crowd growing steadily louder.

Chapter Thirteen - Delphin

I MANAGED TO compose myself. Crusock hovered, looking at me, confusion in his face.

Motion caught my eye. From across the room, Father raced toward us, trident raised. Rage contorted his features into a terrifying mask. I barely recognized him.

Father knocked me out of the way. I smashed into the wall. He circled around and, without a moment's hesitation, stabbed Crusock straight through the chest and out his back. Father yanked his trident out. Blood clouded the water as Crusock made a horrible sound and pitched forward.

Crusock had made my life miserable ever since I could remember. Yet all I felt was a sharp pain of loss as I watched his body float, lifeless.

Father hovered, weapon in hand. His red battle cloak billowed like the blood that still swirled around Crusock as two soldiers took the youth's dead body away. Crusock's parents had died during the Great War. Father had executed Barron. Now the whole family was gone.

I wanted to ask why. But there was no point. I knew the answer. *The rules.* We must always follow the rules, and I'd just broken a cardinal tournament rule.

The crowd remained silent as they watched my father, their regent, twirl his trident clean. He raised his hand and pointed me back to the other warriors.

"Go." That was all he said. My fin stung as I swam back and a small trail of blood followed me, but I'd lived.

The crowd grew restless again, perhaps wondering if the tournament had ended. Father raised his hand to quiet them. He motioned for Krenil to approach and the two spoke privately for a moment before Krenil swam away.

"We must weed out the weak no matter the price! Without *order*, what are we?"

"Nothing!" the crowd roared.

"Without discipline, what will happen?"

"We die!" they screamed.

"Weakness was coddled for generations and look what it brought. The strong will rise with the help of the Tentacle Lord! Now there will be one final sparring match. An honor, to fight me. The one who is most *deserving*…" Father's mouth curled with contempt, "…is my son."

Momentary silence and then the crowd erupted with noise, chattering, cheering, clicking, and speaking all at once. The water buzzed and vibrated with energy, and my teeth hummed in my head.

I looked over at my friend Ilanys. His eyes went wide and a tear bubble popped from his eye.

I sent out a private communication. "Goodbye, Ily," I said. "If you ever see Ariella, tell her I love her."

I should have felt terrified, but I wasn't. Not yet. All I felt was a numb shock that crept up my limbs and settled in my chest. Father didn't even look at me as I swam to the center.

Now, my heart started to pound. Maybe I was wrong? Maybe he just wanted to teach me a lesson, not kill me? The look in his single baleful eye said otherwise.

Krenil rang the sea-gong and Father circled me, face impassive. He thrust forward. Despite my wound, I hadn't lost all nimbleness. Father was a giant compared to me, a battle-scarred warrior who depended on brute force and power. I dodged in time and swam as fast as I could.

Father was quicker than I realized. With my injury, I was no match for him. We did a loop and then he stopped, watching me, tracking his prey. He wasn't tired but my muscles trembled with fatigue.

"Coward," he sent out, a message just for me. "Fight, you impotent worm! Or accept your fate like a man." And he raced toward me. The point of his trident jabbed toward me. I thrust up, just like I had with Crusock. I felt a percussive burst of energy surge through my arms and his trident got diverted up. Father swam, eye narrowed, looking down at his forearms still rippling and pulsing with energy.

For a moment, he paused, and then he smiled. He'd never smiled at me. Not once in my entire life. His eye met mine, and I felt as if he were seeing me for the first time. It made me realize that he'd never looked at me. Maybe he'd never wanted to.

He twirled his trident in his hand, swapping it from right to left, showing off. Then he parried forward and lunged again. I tried to deflect a second time, but he was ready. My trident missed and swooshed through the water. I shifted my fin to the right and narrowly missed being impaled. His trident sunk into the plastered surface.

The moment it got stuck allowed me to reorient. I held my trident up pointed toward his chest. I gave a tentative jab forward, but he blocked me with his forearm.

Father's eye flashed with fury. "Useless!" he shouted. And he raised his trident and bore down toward my throat.

"No!" I cried. Fear, terror, and anger pulsed through my body. I stabbed forward. A powerful current ran through me into my trident. The weapon barely touched his chest, but it emitted a pulse and tone that deafened me. Everything went blue, then white then gray.

When my senses cleared, I watched Father tumble backward, pain wracking his face as he convulsed. The rope holding his seashell patch broke and revealed his blind eye.

At some point, he'd sustained a grievous wound. A jagged scar extended from his eye's inner corner to nose. His eyeball was still intact. The lame, injured eye stared off far to his right, cock-eyed as if it looked directly at me. That eye looked so different from his working eye. It appeared frozen in a contorted expression of pain and fear.

He floated down to the center of the arena and lay unconscious, trident gripped in his massive hand as if he would never let it go. His red battle tunic covered him, now ripped and torn.

What I have done? I thought, stomach roiling.

* * *

"Will he be okay?" I asked for the third time.

Abalon tended to Father in the healing ward. He lay in a bed of sea-silks. His face was pale, almost gray, and for the first time, he looked weak.

"His nervous system has suffered a severe shock." Abalon bustled around gathering together various sea vegetables and herbs. Maybe it was my imagination, but I felt as though she looked at me with new eyes. With caution.

"Will he be well enough to lead the Hunt?" Krenil asked.

Abalon raised her eyebrows. "Absolutely not. He'll be lucky if he lives." She made tiny bunches of herbs wrapped in seaweed.

I turned to Krenil. "What else can we do?"

Krenil shook his head. "I'm no healer. You dealt a grave wound."

"I didn't want this!" I shouted.

Suddenly, a hand shot out and gripped mine. I gasped. Father held my wrist tight, his eyes shot open.

"You fought well. I'm proud," he said. "*You* will lead the Hunt."

"Me? Lead the Hunt? I've never even been on a Hunt!"

Krenil swam forward. "I can lead the Hunt, young master. Don't worry."

"My son will lead the Hunt!" Father raised himself up and shouted. Then he fell back.

Krenil bowed his head. "Yes, your regency. If that's your wish, it shall be done."

He continued to grip my wrist so hard I thought it might snap. "A merman who can wield a trident like that can lead."

"Here, Delphin." Abalon eyed my wounded fin. "You'll be wanting that tended to if you'll be leading your first Hunt."

* * *

Back in my quarters, I flopped onto my sea-silk bed, exhausted. I couldn't sleep. Images from the day tormented me. The crowd's lust for blood. Chrysalis. Crusock dying. Father's disdain… and then his pride in me. I'm not sure which was more difficult.

I wanted to speak to Ariella. Even if I'd been able to sneak away in secret, I didn't have the energy for a long swim. My body, mind, and soul were drained.

Lifting Barron's trident, I twirled it in my hands. Where had the pulses of energy come from? I'd heard of merrow who could transmit with extreme force. It was a lost skill. Nowadays, strength came first, the ability to project intent into our tridents added to their power, but it wasn't the primary force behind the weapons.

A heavy feeling sat in the pit of my stomach. Father wanted me to lead the Hunt and so I would. Now that I had his approval, I suppose I should have been happy. Hadn't this always been what I'd wanted? It was nothing like I expected. Instead of relief or lightness, there was only a heavy sense of dread and responsibility.

* * *

* * *

The next days brought treatment I'd never experienced before. I got offered the fattest fish and ate with the council members. Chrysalis no longer taunted me. When we crossed paths, she looked at me with a dim, uncertain respect and an expression I couldn't read.

I tried to find a moment to sneak away to find Ariella, but it was impossible. I didn't dare.

Ily wouldn't leave me alone. "How did you do it? Will you teach me?" he pleaded.

"I'm not even sure what I did!" I told him in private. What I didn't admit was my suspicion that it had had nothing to do with me at all. It had been thanks to Barron's trident.

Krenil came and collected his loan after the match. *It served you well,* was all he said.

Now I had my larger, much more ornate trident again. I was glad to have it back, but it didn't feel as nimble as Barron's. Father's pride was misplaced. I was a fake and a fraud.

Chapter Fourteen - Delphin

THE DAY OF the Hunt arrived far faster than I'd have liked. Trident clasped in my right hand, I swam with a group of twenty other merrow into the night sea. I sent out a sharp click of sound and waited for it to return. The time it took to echo back would show the size of the space.

Beneath me, the seafloor lay a comforting distance below—perhaps a ten-minute swim. Behind us, I sensed the sea-gate ready to welcome us home. Ahead of me, the click never returned.

The Great Sea.

"Daunting, huh?" Anem, one of the older mermen, said to me. "It goes on forever."

I was used to life in my colony. Walls surrounded me and separated us from the dangers of the open sea. The one time I'd gone with Ariella to Uncle Nebulon's swirl, where I'd found the sheath, we hadn't ventured far. This was something different. Eerie blue light filtered from far up on the surface. Not a moonstone. The moon herself.

"A clear night, good for hunting," Krenil said.

"Don't be disappointed if we find nothing worth taking. Lately, we've encountered many large ones here. Impossible to break through."

I nodded but didn't know what they were talking about. Officially, I was leading this Hunt. Father commanded it. It was a position of honor and prestige. However, I'd never been on a Hunt so I had no clue what to do. I depended on the others to help.

We swam farther into the blue-black water, ascending toward the surface. My heart pounded in my chest. When my head breached, I took rapid gasps in the air, spitting up water. Anem made a pained face and spit out a massive plume of water. The others arrived moments after. No one seemed to enjoy it.

"It burns." I coughed and choked.

Krenil thumped me on the back. He'd adjusted fast.

"Relax and let the air in. You're tensing your throat," he spoke. Spoke! Words out loud. His voice was gravelly, and it seemed an effort for him, but the same words that I would have heard in my mind, I heard in my ears. Like a song. Like echolocation. Vibration. I grinned at him and he smiled.

"Good job leading so far, young master."

I took a few more shaky breaths that became more relaxed. I looked up at... the sky. Points of light shone down. Stars! Ariella told me about them. I whirled around the water until I grew dizzy.

"We can't risk staying on the surface too long," Anem transmitted. I wondered why Anem hadn't spoken like Krenil.

"I—" I started to speak, but the word came out a growl and the rest was just unpleasant noise.

Anem laughed. A musical vibration that tickled the temples of my head.

"It takes practice," he transmitted. "I've never gotten the hang of it. Transmission is faster and more accurate."

There was no time for practice. A thrum traveled through the water, subtle but too large to be a fish. We descended and swam toward its source.

"A boat!" My heart slammed in my chest. Krenil had sent mental pictures of what they looked like.

"Not just any boat, a slow, soft one," Anem replied with a gleeful smile. "Ripe for the taking."

It traveled low in the water.

"Watch and learn," Krenil said. "This is small. We want to conserve our energy. We'll only need five to take it." He pointed to five merrow, and they gathered around him.

Anem was among them, and he gave me an excited grin. "You're going to love this!"

The boat drew closer. As it passed over, the five merrow shot up, tridents held above their heads. Five tridents hit the hull of the boat. Cracks appeared. In a frenzy of bubbles, they hit again and again. The boat stopped buzzing. Moments later, the water was filled with debris... and humans.

Krenil's face lit up with wicked glee as over twenty humans thrashed in the water as the boat capsized. "Oh, so many! What a wonderful surprise!"

Most couldn't swim. Krenil jabbed one in the thigh just enough to wound it.

"This is a Hunt?" I asked. The sight of blood in the water made me nauseous. No one heard my question. Like sharks possessed with blood lust, they played with their prey.

Anem grabbed one man and pulled him under. Then he allowed the man to swim to the surface before he pulled the man under again. Why didn't he just put the being out of his misery? Bile collected at the back of my throat.

This was supposed to be an honor? I was supposed to lead these? Anem looked over and narrowed his eyes. If I didn't take part, it would get back to my father. He'd done me a great honor allowing me to lead.

Not far above, a pair of bare, muscular legs kicked. I swam up. I couldn't bear to drag him down into the water. Although humans couldn't transmit to each other, I could hear and feel their thoughts. I sensed panic, misery, and fright. It filled the water like a miasma. I would kill this one quick, put him out of its misery.

Trident set forth before me, I swam up, ready to make a clean kill. Somehow the youth, and it was a youth, a male about my age, sensed me. He whirled around in the water and I missed, only managing to nick his calf from behind. I caught a quick flash of his worried face. He looked familiar.

The boy moved fast for a human. He grabbed a piece of scrap wood and sunk his face in the water, trying to locate the source of attack. Amidst all the bubbles and debris, I could see him best using my echolocation. He looked like the boy from the photo! That couldn't be, could it?

I swam closer until we were face-to-face. Our eyes locked. My throat tightened. Time slowed. The boy had the face of a warrior and a prince, all in one. Delicate lashes fluttered like tiny fish in front of wide, innocent eyes, one brown and one green. Even more handsome than his photo. A story come to life.

The boy reached out and grabbed me. For a moment, I thought he was attacking. But he clutched me around my torso. He thought I was helping him.

As the boy's hands touched his chest, images from another life flashed through my mind as our bodies connected. Life on the surface. Another world that was dry. And boiling hot.

Without considering the implications, I grabbed the boy and swam away unnoticed through the chaos and wreckage.

Chapter Fifteen - Delphin

NOW WE WERE alone, Elias and me. *Elias.* I'd picked up his name and random flashes of images. A sinking boat. A terrible voyage. I swam at the surface far from the wreckage. Elias lay slumped half-conscious and waterlogged against my shoulder.

I shuddered with anguish as I thought of the carnage I'd witnessed. It made me ashamed to be a merman. Now I understood why Ariella felt the way she did.

All this time, I'd thought humans were stupid and ignorant. That they had no complex emotions: eat, breed, and sleep. It wasn't true. Humans were not so unlike us. They felt pain, sadness, and fear. They had pods and people they loved. I'd seen it through Elias.

The sea was black and filled with strong currents in this area. Giant fronds of brown kelp whipped back and forth. Something hit me in the head and I spun around. Just a piece of wood.

Humans needed air. Humans needed land. Here we were in the middle of the sea with the human's boat destroyed. A wind came up and from behind the clouds, the moon beamed down. Off in the distance lay a rocky island.

"Delphin!" A group of voices transmitted loudly in the distance. The Hunt must have ended. If they found me, they would kill the human. And the fact that I was protecting the boy? Father's reaction when I spared Crusock flashed through my mind.

Whatever the punishment, it would be severe for us both. Humans were our enemies. They were one of the main reasons we'd been driven to near extinction. All the pride that Father had gained in me from the tournament would be dissolved in an instant.

Elias lost consciousness, and I sang to him. I wasn't sure if a human would hear the transmission. But the boy did. His eyes opened wide, and they met mine. Elias gazed at me in wonder, mumbling something in a language I couldn't yet understand.

I pulled him through a rocky shoal until the water became too shallow.

He lost consciousness again, and I sang something stronger, drawing on my heart song, until Elias opened his eyes again. A smile played across his face. The human reached out and caressed my face, speaking his strange language.

Elias' legs shook, but he stood and stumbled through the rocks onto the pebbled beach. He sunk to his knees, chest heaving. Would he be okay? Now that he had air was that all that he needed?

I'd been gone too long. I had to get back. Time to implement my plan. I picked up a large stone, braced myself, and smashed it hard against my temple.

My vision wavered. For a moment, I thought I'd overdone it. Seawater stung the open wound. I regained my equilibrium and slid down into the night water. Fearful of sharks, I swam fast toward my pod's transmissions. Soon I found them.

Krenil rushed to me when he saw the blood oozing from my temple. I sealed my mind tight, ready to make up the story images I'd grown adept at spinning. Story lies that sometimes even I believed to be true.

"I killed two humans, then a giant piece of hull smashed into me and knocked me out. A current grabbed me. I woke up when I heard you all calling."

Krenil and Anem's faces paled. While I couldn't read their thoughts, I imagined what they might be. If I got lost on my first Hunt, it might not have gone well for them. Now, if I'd died, and they'd returned with my body… Father might have celebrated my courage.

"It was my fault. I'll tell Father that. Don't fret." After all the suffering I'd witnessed, I didn't want to cause more. Even though I still couldn't remove the memory of Krenil's broad grin as he disemboweled one human after the next. With no regard for age, sex… or anything.

On the way back, I couldn't help but ask, "Krenil, when you're hunting the humans, do you sometimes see things… transmissions?"

Krenil shook his head. "I used to at the start. Nothing sophisticated —only what you'd expect from a human. Still unpleasant though. I'll teach you how to shut out the noise. Next time."

* * *

* * *

After our tournament and successful Hunt, the festive mood calmed as merrow got back to work. Father showed signs of improvement but remained weak. When he saw my head wound, he clenched his fist and pounded his breast.

"That's my son!" he said. "That's my warrior!"

Abalon stopped him.

Meanwhile, Ariella was not forgotten, Krenil had soldiers out looking for her non-stop. It seemed though that they'd relaxed their surveillance of me. I worried about her. It had been days now.

Was she lonely? Was she frightened? I wanted to tell her about Elias. I gazed at his photo whenever I got the chance. I remembered the wonderful feeling of his body warm and wet beneath my hands. I wondered and worried about how he was doing, alone on that barren island.

During sleep-time, I took a risk and snuck through the side passages. Several times, I circled around and back to make sure I wasn't followed. Once I was satisfied, I sped toward the area where I'd last seen our uncle and sent out a gentle probe.

Moments later, Ariella threw her arms around me in a flurry of bubbles. She looked fabulous.

"Ariella, how are you?"

"Brother, I wish they had chosen me for sacrifice years ago!" Ariella smiled. "I adore the exile lifestyle. It suits me, don't you think?" She pouted and dropped into a sexy pose.

I burst into laughter but grew serious. "Krenil is still looking for you," I warned.

Ariella shrugged. "Stuff him. I don't care. Good luck finding me here. When we finish rebuilding the old palace wards, it'll be impossible."

"Where's Uncle Nebulon? What do you do all day?"

"Uncle is sleeping. I spend most of my time in the library studying scrolls. No one bothers me. Uncle Nebulon lets me do what I want, when I want. We have plenty of food. Maybe it's not so varied as back in the pod, but it could be worse all things considered."

I told her about the tournament and then the Hunt. Throughout my tale, her eyes got wider and wider. "This could be a story from a story shell! You're pulling my fin, aren't you?"

I shook my head. "It's all true. I've fallen in love with a human boy. His name is Elias. He's the boy from the photo! Ariella, you see it must be destiny, fate. I'm responsible for him. I fear harm will come to him alone on that island. What do they eat?"

Ariella bit her lip. "I don't know. Fish?"

That made me feel somewhat better. "There were plenty of fish around the island for him to catch."

"But humans must drink, too. They can't absorb water from their skin."

"He's on an island surrounded by water."

"No, they need different water. It's strange. I think it falls from the sky."

"Maybe he's fine, but I'm… worried."

"Go! See him. Not now. Wait until morning. When you return, stay here with me."

"You mean for good?"

Ariella nodded. "Do you want to live in the pod with all its rules and regulations? Delph, things used to be very different. There are secrets in those scrolls that can change everything for the better. Once upon a time, we lived a beautiful, magical life beneath the sea. We can have all that again, I know it! I just need to learn more."

Ariella was as in love with her scrolls as I was with the human boy and yet I wasn't sure I was ready to live life as an exile.

"They're having dinner in my honor tomorrow night. Father is giving me more and more responsibilities. I will be Regent one day, you know. I'll change the rules we don't like." I didn't dare tell her my most secret fantasy. In my wildest dreams, I ruled our pod… with Elias at my side. Just like the story shell.

"Is Father *dying*?"

I shook my head. "No, but since the tournament, he has confidence in me. Ariella, once he trusts me even more, I'll have him pardon you. You could come back."

"I don't *want* to come back."

"Not even to see Father?"

"Delph, he sacrificed me!"

"That wasn't his fault; it was just bad luck. He was just following the rules."

"I'll make you a deal. If you can get him to pardon me *and* drop the stupid rule about visiting the forbidden areas, I'll consider coming back."

That sounded like a lot at once, even to me. "I'll get them to pardon you. When you come back, we can change the rules about the old areas. I need you to explain the scrolls' importance. Deal?"

Ariella folded her arms. She cocked her head. "Oh, fine, a deal, I suppose." She kissed me on the cheek. "Now I have more research to do. You'd be amazed at what I'm finding."

Chapter Sixteen - Delphin

FATHER LAY ON the sea-silk bed while Abalon handed him engraved pieces of coral, each one with a new proposed rule. When he saw me, his face broke into a smile.

It made my insides shake and shiver. It was as if I'd woken up and found myself with a new father. I don't remember ever having received anything from him except scowls and frowns.

His new approval of me made me somewhat nervous. Bound by luck and lies, I felt it could crash down at any moment.

"I'm sorry I'm early, Father."

He waved me in and put aside his coral. "Not at all, I'm glad you're here. It will give me a chance to explain how council meetings work."

"Are those all new rules?" I pointed to the engraved pieces of coral.

Father nodded. "Some of them I approve outright. Others we'll discuss during the meeting."

"Don't we already have enough? Regulations, I mean."

Father drew me closer. "There's something you need to understand about merrow. We are creatures of the water. Things are constantly in motion. There's nothing for us to grasp onto. Rules, regulations, and dictates are all we have. Without them, we'd become like jellyfish. No structure! No measure of who we are or what we could be! Do you understand?"

I nodded. "Now that I'm attending council meetings, will I be able to propose new rules?"

A twinkle appeared in Father's eye. "Krenil has the best mind for rules of anyone. But all council members are eligible."

"Do you approve all of Krenil's rules and regulations?"

Father laughed. "Absolutely not. Krenil has a sharp mind, but he doesn't understand the big picture. As Regent, that's my duty. What's your proposal? The way a rule gets crafted is key."

"It's about Ariella." I knotted my hands at the front of my chest. "I thought there might be some rule that spares her."

Father's face darkened. "It pained me to see her chosen. However, it would not be proper to create a rule just to bend situations to our favor. Rules and regulations are sacred!"

"But you're Regent."

"Sacred! They're the bones of merrow society."

"Your Regency." Abalon swam to Father's side. "Best that you don't upset yourself." She glared at me over her shoulder.

"I'm sorry, Sir. It's just she's my sister. I love her and I don't want to lose her. We need her here."

Father's face softened. "Krenil knows all the ins and outs of our rules and regulations. We *cannot* create a rule. However, perhaps there's some facet that he overlooked that might help her."

* * *

Each council member held a luma crystal. Krenil hovered on my right side. Big, barrel-chested Flotsam, Finner, and Teomath swam next to him.

This was the protocol: If a member wanted to initiate a topic, they placed the crystal in the giant, golden clamshell that sat in the center. Father opened the meeting.

"It's unfortunate we can't meet in our regular chambers, however, I'm told that moving might kill me. Is that so, Abalon?" Father emitted a sour laugh.

Abalon flushed. "Best not take the risk, Your Regency."

Normally, Abalon wouldn't be included in a meeting. She remained to tend to Father if he needed her. Whatever I'd done to him had really messed him up. He still hadn't regained mobility.

I rolled the luma crystal back-and-forth between my fingers and then stopped when I saw Father watching.

"Let us begin," Father said and looked at me.

Father placed his crystal down before anyone else had the chance. Not that I planned on it.

"First order of business. Should I die, my son, Delphin, will become Regent."

"Your Regency, he's not an initiated male."

I glared at Krenil. He knew that my showing at the tournament qualified me for initiation! I'd already gone on my first Hunt! He shot me an apologetic smile.

"Not true. His performance in the tournament qualified him despite his age and inexperience. You would act as his guide. Just as you have to me. Not that I expect this to happen. Best to always be prepared."

An awkward silence fell over the room. "Oh, stop with the long faces," Father said. "I'll be fine."

After a long pause, Krenil put a crystal in the center. "Second order of business: Ariella. She's not been found. She's in serious breach of her duties. I know we all want sacrifices to happen on a schedule that pleases our Tentacle Lord. This threatens to put us behind."

Father shifted, a pained expression on his face. "Krenil, is it possible there's some facet to this you've overlooked? We want to uphold the rules, and yet the fact that she is my daughter puts us all in an awkward position."

"Sir, I'm glad you asked. I've wanted to discuss the matter myself. Now, if Ariella had been betrothed to an immune subject, she would *not* have been subject to sacrifice."

This was news to me.

Krenil continued, "Ariella and I had discussed marriage prior to her unfortunate selection. We were enamored with one another and practically betrothed."

I listened to Krenil, astonished. This was a complete lie.

"Perhaps we might hold another Sacrifice and select a replacement merrow to appease our Tentacle Lord? Your Regency has the power to marry Ariella and me in absentia. Once she is found, she would no longer be subject to the sacrificial order because of our marriage."

Krenil shot me a pleased wink. I returned an uncertain smile. I felt positive Ariella would rather be sacrificed to the Tentacle Lord than marry Krenil. However, it didn't seem fair to Krenil. If not for him, I'd probably be dead. I felt the horrible feeling that I was about to be caught in the middle of a war between my most staunch supporter and my sister.

On my way out, Krenil grabbed my arm. "Young Master, you'll tell Ariella that we have spared her the next time you see her, won't you?"

"I don't know where she is. I told you." I felt bad lying to him, but as much a friend as he was, my ultimate loyalty lay with Ariella.

"Of course." Krenil gave me a closed-mouth smile and a wink. "It would be treason if you spoke to her. However, if someone saw her... it would make sense to tell her, wouldn't it?"

"Yes," I said.

Krenil nodded. "Good night, Young Master."

Chapter Seventeen - Delphin

THAT NIGHT, I could not sleep. Finally, I decided to break the news to Ariella. I hoped she'd see reason. A pardon was what she wanted... Well, now she had one. But oh, boy, she would not like the terms.

Krenil must have sent extra eyes to watch me. Teomath, Father's best and meanest soldier, followed. I put on a burst of speed and was happy to note that whatever Abalon gave me had healed my wound. Teomath knew my strengths. He swam almost as fast as me.

Almost.

Soon I'd outpaced him. It had not been easy. Now I was lost. I swam near the secret exit to the Great Sea. Filtered sunlight illuminated the water. It was just past dawn. My mind turned to Elias.

A guilty feeling gathered in my stomach. I'd been so busy the last couple of days I'd never found the opportunity to check up on him. How was he doing on the island? It was early. I didn't want to wake Ariella. In truth, I didn't relish delivering the news about Krenil. Without considering the danger, I swam through the crevasse.

I'd never swam out into the Great Sea on my own. Tango swam behind, chattering nervously. Being a rescue, Tango feared the open water. He preferred to stay in the pod with me.

"Calm, calm, okay, it's okay." I reached out and stroked Tango's silky smooth flank. Whether Tango understood language, I wasn't sure, but he understood my intent. Everything would be okay.

The water changed from a deep-blue so dark it was almost black to light-blue and then aquamarine. A golden sunrise spread her giant arms of light—beams that were so broad they looked like columns hugging sky to water.

Deep water gave way to shallow coral as I neared the island where I'd left Elias. I tried to remember everything I knew about humans.

Unlike merrow, they couldn't absorb water through their skin. Would there have been water on the island? Perhaps water had fallen from the above place Ariella mentioned. Clouds. The sky. I swam faster. Tango matched my pace, chattering again as he picked up my anxiety. This time, I didn't attempt to calm my dolphin companion. It would have been no use. I was too agitated to conjure calming images.

I patted Tango on his floppy dorsal fin and continued. We zoomed over coral as we played the game he loved. I caught up to Tango and grabbed his fin. We sliced through the water.

Soon we arrived at the island's shallows. My heart pounded with exertion and excitement. I broke the surface and found the area where I'd last seen Elias. A rogue wave broke, catching me off guard and nearly sending me sprawling into the barnacle- and sea-urchin-filled shoal.

It wasn't a large island. It had a pebble beach. Scrubby vegetations led up a steep incline. I spotted a cliffside far above the sand and surf.

Flipping onto my back, I let the current take me along the outside ring of the island past the point where fine pebbles turned to rock. There I spotted him. He stood, bare-chested, on a ridge looking across the island at the ocean on the other side. The muscles in his back rippled as he struggled to extricate something from beneath a rock.

Elias yanked hard and a triumphant smile spread across his face as he made progress at freeing the item. My heart quickened. I'd never seen him smile. His face glowed. Elias was beautiful. He struggled with what appeared to be a piece of fabric. Tango surfaced and squeaked at me.

"Shh!" I patted his flank.

Elias turned his head toward the sea. I submerged. When I peered back up, he'd returned to his struggle.

What is he doing?

I continued to watch, partly out of curiosity and partly because I couldn't stop watching him. With his face profiled in the morning sun, he reminded me of a statue from the forbidden areas. A warrior prince. Fine hairs on his arms glowed in the rising sun.

I saved a life. I saved his life, and he doesn't even know it. Probably never will.

The thought filled me with confusion. We weren't supposed to mix with humans—only to kill them. I'd never heard of anyone interacting with a human aside from the Hunts. My wants were constantly at odds with my pod.

Elias yanked the canvas sheet free. He hoisted it above his head and waved it back and forth, shouting.

I dove beneath the water and raced around the other side. Tango could barely keep up. When I reached the other side, I saw it. A small boat sat far on the horizon. I didn't know much about boats except that they provided safety to humans. Of course! Elias needed help from his own kind.

I turned back toward the island. I couldn't see Elias from this vantage point, and with the sun at its current angle, I found it doubtful anyone from the boat would see him. Somehow, I needed to help. I swam to the side of the island where the sun shone its brightest.

My plan was risky. I needed to make sure I wasn't spotted. I angled my tail so it caught the sun's rays. Blinding light glittered and reflected off my scales into the sky. Back and forth I waved my tail, allowing the sun to glint and glimmer. Soon the boat changed course. I sunk back into the water and swam around the other side.

Elias shouted in his human language as he waved his arms. He clambered down off the rock as a smaller boat buzzed toward the island.

When they entered the harbor, my blood chilled. Even from my vantage hidden behind a rock in the water, I sensed something wrong. A dark energy emanated from the men, as obvious as the stench of forgotten fish rotting beneath the sea.

There were three of them. The driver wore an odd black plastic object that hid his eyes. Embedded in its sides were tiny gemstones. From the quality of their sparkles, it appeared that the gems were some quartz-like material—not true gems like we had in our pod. The driver was the biggest of the three. He had a broad wrinkled forehead and a piece of blue cloth tied around his head.

The two men in the back were younger, not much older than the boy on the island in human years. They had dark-ringed eyes and hostile, slumped postures.

When the boat landed, the two men in back grabbed shiny black objects. Weapons. Not unlike our tridents except from what I'd learned, these were useless beneath the surface. *Guns.* That was what they were called.

If we spotted guns on a vessel, Krenil told me we were to call off a Hunt immediately. I didn't know how they worked. Apparently, they were deadly. The man with the hidden eyes shouted. Elias dropped to his knees in the sand, hands behind his head.

The two younger men laughed as they whipped the gun across Elias' face. Tear bubbles popped from my eyes. Why were they hurting him? The man forced Elias to his feet, made him spread his legs and searched his body. Then they took a length of rope, bound his hands, and dragged him out to the small boat and tossed him in.

I swam closer to their craft, not sure what to do. Perhaps I could sink it? But Elias might come to harm. On the other hand, I could try and rescue him again. But these men had guns. We might both be killed.

I poked my head above the water. The man with hidden eyes sucked on a slender, brown stick. White clouds puffed into the air. Meanwhile, the two younger guys climbed the path that led to the cliff. When they returned, they carried a wooden crate and spoke with much excitement, pointing back and forth. They got back in the small boat and launched off.

"Tango!" I transmitted, noticing that he hadn't followed me. Maybe he found some fish to chase? It seemed everything was snarled and confused all at once. The men forced Elias onto the larger boat. Then two other men hoisted up the crate.

I couldn't see what was happening to Elias. But I heard a terrible commotion—shouts and nasty laughter.

The three men got back into the boat without Elias and returned to the island. I stayed put, wracking my brain for a solution. It was my fault that Elias ended up with these men!

The sun rose higher. Soon I'd be missed back at the pod and I still needed to speak to Ariella.

Elias helped the two younger men move the boat's cargo. Maybe he didn't move it fast enough or said something they didn't like. One of them raised his fist and smashed Elias in the nose. Blood sprayed and I felt the boy's pain shoot across the ocean and into my heart.

"I will return and save you! Don't worry. Be calm," I transmitted as hard as I could. Elias glanced in my direction. Had he heard me? I froze as we locked eyes. Elias' mouth fell open.

When Elias had seen me last, he'd been half-drowned and drunk with fear. But this time? This time, a human had seen me for certain. A thrill ran through my heart and my chest flooded with warmth. I descended into the ocean.

Chapter Eighteen - Delphin

SWIMMING TO MEET Krenil the next day, I noticed changes. There were more builders. In fact, a few merrow who were normally soldiers worked as makeshift builders. I'd hardly slept. I couldn't stop thinking of Elias and the mess I'd gotten him in. I'd killed Barron. I would *not* let Elias die too.

I met Krenil in his chambers. For as long as I could remember, there had always been someone held in the nearby cell, waiting for sacrifice. It felt strange to see it empty, gate open. It felt even stranger to think that this cell waited for Ariella.

"Young Master, I'm worried for Ariella. Her marriage opportunity will expire if she doesn't present herself before the next moon. Do you think she realizes this?"

"I—"

"Rumor is that your sister has a confidant who may have had difficulty seeing her because of heightened security. Unfortunately, we're falling behind on repairs to corridors and walls and won't be able to watch so closely."

I'd never seen this side of Krenil. Sneaky. Not saying what he really meant. It made me very nervous. He must know I was visiting Ariella. Why not just come out and say it?

Anyway, I got the message. Soldiers wouldn't interfere with me finding my sister. When I returned to my chambers, Finner was no longer lurking. I was about to head off when two soldiers arrived at my quarters. Was Krenil messing with me?

"Young Master, come with me, please. The Regent wishes to see you. It's urgent." The soldiers led me into the main hall and I followed.

Perhaps Krenil read my thoughts somehow. I'd been found out. They knew about Elias. About everything.

Bustle and commotion awaited me when I entered the main passage. Merrow stopped their work and headed for the arena.

Can I break away and make a run for it?

No. The hallways teemed with merrow.

I'd never make it through before being captured. Anyway, although life as an exile seemed to suit Ariella, I wasn't sure it would suit me. I needed fellow merrow. I enjoyed the hum and bustle of our pod.

The solider led me toward the healing quarters and I braced myself for Father's rage. When I arrived, Krenil and Abalon swam by Father's side. Father's face was gray.

"He's here, Your Regency," Abalon said.

"What happened?" I asked.

Abalon looked flustered. "He worsened during the night. His heart, I think. He's entire nervous system has never been right since..."

"My son." He raised his hand into a fist. "My warrior. I'm dying."

"Now, now. There's no need to get hasty," Abalon said.

"It's true. If not now, soon, I think. I want to make arrangements. Come closer."

I swam to his side, and he grabbed my hand.

"I must appoint a new Regent."

"Your Regency." Krenil bowed. "I'm here to serve."

"You are a valued confidant, Krenil. Delphin will find you as helpful to him as you were to me."

Krenil's face wavered. "Sir, with my utmost respect, might I suggest that he's young. I can serve as Regent until we ensure—"

"Krenil, you've already shared your feelings. My son is young, but he's proven himself in battle. He is my son. He will serve as Regent in my place."

That night, just as I drifted off into a restless slumber, the crystal bells rang. Before I was born, they were meant as a warning we were under attack. Now they could only mean one thing: Father had died.

Chapter Nineteen - Delphin

THE BELLS WERE still ringing when I grabbed my trident and snuck off. There was no more putting it off: I *had* to find Ariella. She needed to know that Father had died.

Winding my way into the abandoned area, tear bubbles sprouted from my eyes. My entire life, Father and I had been at odds. It felt ironic and tragic that the one deed I'd done in my entire life that made him proud of me had also killed him.

As I grew closer to the abandoned palace, I turned back and sent out a burst of echolocation every so often to make certain I wasn't followed. I found Ariella in the library, flew into her arms, and burst violent sobs.

"Delphin! My poor, sweet Delphin, what's wrong?"

"Father died, and I killed him. First Barron and now Father. Elias may be dead too by now!"

She paused, and I felt her shiver. Her heart energy poured out. "That stupid, stupid man," she said through tears. "The customs he promoted are *not* your fault. You did not kill him. His rules and ridiculous regulations did!" She forced me back and looked me in the eye. "You realize that, don't you?"

Maybe part of me did. I tried to. "I can still feel the moment when the trident struck him. I was so scared. So angry. I *wanted* to hurt him. I just never thought that—"

"Of course, you wanted to hurt him! You said he tried to kill you. Remember? Tell me you haven't forgotten that part? If he knew about your love for the human boy, for other boys, he'd kill you right now if he had the chance. Don't forget that, Delphin. In my own way, I grieve Father too. But he brought this all upon himself. Now that you're Regent... well, it's time to make changes."

"I have news," I said with a soft voice. "They granted you a pardon."

"Before Father died?"

I nodded. "There were conditions, though."

Ariella's smile disappeared. "Such as?" She folded her arms.

"That you marry Krenil."

Ariella went silent for a moment. I thought she'd be very upset. Instead, she burst into laughter. She laughed so hard I thought she might burst her fin. Finally, when she was able to speak, she said one word: "Never."

"I knew you'd take it well."

"And I'll tell you something else," she said. "I think Krenil orchestrated the whole thing! I think he got me chosen for sacrifice. Think about it: Orbin, Seawrack, and Alec. They all crossed Krenil. Orbin wanted to join Father's council. Krenil couldn't stand him. Nevertheless, Orbin might have succeeded if he hadn't been 'chosen.' Alec openly defied Krenil in front of hundreds of workers! What happens? Oh, he's off for sacrifice."

"How would Krenil organize that?"

"He was the one handing out the shells. Remember how he'd play all those tricks for us when we were small fry? Pulling things out of our ears, making shells appear in his hand from nowhere? He's up to tricks again."

"Solitude is making you paranoid, Sister." I swam and placed my hand on her cheek. "Can you blame Krenil for being enamored with you? That's all this is about. His flame will fade."

"If you believe that, you don't understand men. Delphin, has your passion for Elias faded? Or gotten stronger with his absence?"

Blood rushed to my face. I could barely stop thinking about him. How handsome he looked when he smiled. How warm his back felt pressed against my chest. Father's death intensified my feelings in a strange way.

Uncle Nebulon swam in, eyes bloodshot and bleary.

"You heard about Father?" I asked, mistaking his haggard expression for grief.

He rubbed his eyes. "Heard what? I just woke up. What's going on with that mussel head now?"

"He died. My trident wound killed him."

Nebulon nodded. "Well, you can't say he didn't have it coming."

"You're both so heartless."

Uncle Nebulon shrugged. "He was a bastard. It seems only fair that he be killed with Barron's trident. Speaking of which, where is it?"

I flushed. "Krenil took it back. He wouldn't admit to it, but I think he added some magic to the trident to make it more powerful. If I had to fight Father again with *this* trident, I don't think I'd do so well, handsome though it may be."

"That's your trident? Let me see."

I held it up closer to the dim light that emanated from the few working crystals that remained. It sparkled and shone, impressive, handsome.

"May I?" Uncle came and touched my trident. "Who gave you this?"

"Krenil. I've never seen one like it. It was his gift to me long ago."

Uncle Nebulon snorted and laughed. "A rather poison gift, I'd say."

I nodded. "It made me more of a target. Other merrow were envious. I don't care. I love the way the metal shines."

"Well." Uncle Nebulon folded his arms. "They need not have been jealous. It's pretty, true. But it's a piece of utter junk. I bet it has a core of bone. It was built to *prevent* injury,"

"A trident to prevent injury?" Ariella cocked her head. "Now that I've never heard. Why would someone do that?"

"The theater I've told you about, Ariella. Do you think they used real tridents for their performances? No. No. They forged special tridents. Beautiful, but just for show."

I clutched my trident tighter. "What are you talking about?"

Ariella turned to me. "Generations ago, they put on these spectacles. Merrow pretended they were characters in stories and reenacted them."

"Like the story shells I've found?"

Uncle Nebulon nodded. "Your trident is ornamental. A toy. Were you able to transmit through it at all?"

I nodded. "Weakly, but yes."

"You must be powerful to penetrate your force through that thick thing."

"I don't believe you. Are you jealous of my weapon too, Uncle? Is this some trick?"

"Uncle Nebulon sighed. "You've spent too much time with Krenil. Here." He offered his trident. Similar to Barron's although a bit more beat-up, it was a traditional, silver weapon. My eyes widened. "That's against the rules. I can't use your trident!"

Uncle Nebulon scoffed. "Another one of Krenil's rules, I'm guessing? Well, he's not here. I'm not giving it to you for good. Try it."

He shoved it toward me. I looked at him, stunned.

"Oh, come on!" He forced it in my left hand. A tingle surged through my fingers at the touch of the metal, much as Barron's trident had.

Uncle Nebulon pointed to a mound of rubble that obscured several frescoes. "Aim my trident at that."

Wanting to make sure Uncle Nebulon didn't pull some trick, I put my trident down far from him. He laughed.

"Please, boy!" He shook his head. "Unless I want to put on a show, I have no desire to take your silly toy weapon."

I glared and swam toward the pile of rocks. I raised Uncle Nebulon's trident. It felt light and insubstantial in my hands, much as Barron's had.

"Think of something that makes you angry!" Uncle commanded.

I thought of Elias, captured because of me. Hurt by the men in the boat. A buzzing sensation started in the center of my body and surged out into the metal. When I thrust forward and the tip of the trident hit, the mound of rubble exploded outward. The force pushed a current of water against the frescoed wall that echoed back and sent the three of us tumbling to the floor; an incoherent mound of fins and flesh.

* * *

Once we'd recovered, Uncle Nebulon blocked my way. "My trident?" He held out his hand.

"No, I need it!" I said. "If Krenil lied to me all these years, I don't know what I'll do."

"It's not yours to take." He grabbed it from me. "Besides, you need to learn to contain your power."

"There's no *if* about it, Brother." Ariella shook her head. "Krenil is a scoundrel. He gave you Barron's trident, knowing you *were* powerful. How did you end up fighting Father, anyway?"

I thought of the whispered exchanges I'd witnessed at the tournament.

"Krenil helped me. He was my friend, my mentor. He protected me from Father. He deserves the chance to explain himself."

"What was the price of his protection?" Uncle Nebulon said.

"Ariella, we need to do something. Uncle Nebulon, come with me!"

Uncle Nebulon turned and began to swim away.

"Wait! Where are you going?"

"To do what I'd advise *you* do. Turn your back on this. They are corrupt. They will always be corrupt. Let them destroy themselves!"

I turned to Ariella. "They're all we have left. What will happen to merrow if we just… abandon them?"

"I don't know. There may be answers in the library." She fidgeted. "Uncle is right. Don't go, Delphin. Stay with us." Uncle Nebulon had already disappeared into the shadows.

Picking up my trident, I turned away. "No. Now that Father is dead, I am Regent, at least for now. If Krenil lied to me all this time, then he needs to be punished. There are rules. He broke them."

Chapter Twenty - Elias

"WHERE DID YOU come from, kid?" A bearded man with cragged teeth loomed over Elias.

Elias realized he'd made a huge mistake in flagging down the boat. Yet what choice had there been? He wouldn't have lasted much longer on that blasted island alone.

"I told you… we were trying to cross from Fahad to Italy. There were forty of us in one small boat."

The man named Silas squatted in front of him. Elias caught a whiff of cheap Egyptian olives and sweat.

"How did you get on the island?"

"I—" He remembered a young man's strong arms wrapped around his torso, violet eyes. Dragged up toward the surface then onto the island.

"I swam… passed out, got lucky. Did you see anyone else… out there?" Elias motioned out to the water as he thought of his mother and sister.

Silas narrowed his eyes. "Are there more of you?"

"No," Elias blurted.

"Why shouldn't I dump you back in the ocean where I found you?" Silas scowled.

"I spent a summer on my uncle's boat. I'll work until we get to the next port."

"Next port?" Silas let out a strange bark of a laugh. "We don't need another crew member. What makes you think we're offering you a ride? You've already seen too much."

"I've seen nothing!" Elias said, eyes wide. Had he? He thought of the boy with the body that was half-fish half-man.

"You know what we're looking for."

"A boat… a yacht. Yeah, I heard that… but there must be millions and I don't care. You have my word. I know how to fix things… your engine… it's running rough, no?"

He'd spent hours helping his uncle fix up his fishing boat one summer. He'd never been on a boat this large, but he knew what engines sounded like and this one didn't sound right. It rumbled and rattled the entire structure of the vessel… probably not operating on all cylinders.

If that's what the problem was, he doubted he'd be able to fix it on his own and without parts. Maybe it would buy him time though.

Another guy, his name was Reht, stood at the front of the vessel. His long, dark hair fluttered in the wind as he scanned the ocean with a pair of binoculars. Elias had heard they were looking for a certain yacht. The boat trundled slowly through the waves. Their passage almost felt aimless.

Silas sneered. "You wanna see it?" He hooked his hands into his belt loops. Elias swallowed, not sure where things were headed. "Then you tell me what needs fixing." He grabbed Elias by the arm.

"Can you untie me at least?"

"No," Silas said as he forced him to follow. Elias shuffled to the hatch that led down a ladder to the engine room. It gave an angry shriek as Silas flipped it back, slamming against the metal hull with a dull thud. Elias' eyes widened.

Unlike the beat-up hull of the vessel, the engine appeared shiny, brand new and enormous. It throbbed with power. The boat didn't shake because there was something wrong it. They'd installed an engine much more powerful than the vessel warranted. He thought back to the name of the boat. *The Wolf.*

These men were pirates. The beat-up fishing vessel was their disguise, but no doubt she could travel fast when needed.

"Still want to fix our engine?" Silas laughed.

"Impressive," Elias said. His mouth went dry and pasty. He felt trapped between the desire to get off this boat and wanting to prove himself so they wouldn't toss him to drown or be eaten by sharks. Elias glanced out at the blue sea. It lay impassive, waiting.

"Where's your friend?" Silas asked.

"Friend? I have no friend," he said. But his heart leaped. He'd decided the teen in the ocean— the boy with the violet eyes—had been an illusion. But maybe Silas had seen him?

Silas shrugged. "He'll be dead by night if he ain't already."

How many nights had it been since their boat capsized? What did that mean for his mother and sister? He looked down at the rusty deck, gritting his teeth.

"Silas!" Reht shouted. "Forty-five degrees!" Reht held out the binoculars. Silas strode across the deck and snatched the binoculars from Reht's hand, pressing them to his eyes.

"Your eyes aren't worth a damn," Silas said as he adjusted the focus.

Reht bit his lip and said nothing. "Oh yeah, baby, baby come to daddy," Silas continued. "Omar!" he shouted and whistled. He spun his hand in a circle and pointed starboard. Out on the horizon—a distant white speck.

Elias got thrown to the deck as *The Wolf* took off. Today the ocean was calm, but at this speed, each swell slammed his body hard to the deck. He shuffled crab-like and pushed his back against the deck rail. With his legs tied, it was hard to brace himself and he grew sore from the effort.

Silas and Reht went below, grabbing hold of the rails to keep from falling. They returned with an older, grizzled man. His name was Pavel. Omar, a tall, lean guy about the same age as Reht joined seconds later.

All four of them held AK-47 machine guns. Reht smiled and stuck out his tongue, shaking saltwater out of his windblown hair in wild excitement. He reminded Elias of his father. Hungry for conflict, desperate to prove himself. It seemed Elias had escaped a desert war only to find himself in a new war on the water.

Chapter Twenty-One - Delphin

MY PULSE THROBBED in my head as I swam past rows of merrow. A few looked up and offered nods of acknowledgment, commiseration, and here and there—wonder. It had been no secret I'd once been a disappointment to Father.

Most though, didn't notice me pass. They were too busy chipping away—adding to the Hall of Order. There were thousands of rules inscribed and more added every day. Soon the passage would be extended.

I swam past section after section of rules, scanning for one that might still my mind or help with this horrible situation. Moments later, I jumped at the hand on my shoulder.

"Ah, Young Master, how are you holding up?" Krenil said. "It's been quite a shock, hasn't it?"

I brushed his hand from my shoulder. "Is it true? Did you know my trident was worthless? Did you rig Ariella's selection shell?"

Krenil's face paled. "Young Master!"

Perhaps it would have been wiser for me to watch and wait or to come up with a scheme to catch him. But seeing him brought everything flooding out. I couldn't hold back. Why hadn't I noticed before—the oily quality of his smile? A smile that never reached his eyes. His perfect teeth, meticulously lined razor-sharp points that glinted in a straight line.

"You poor boy. Your father's death has shaken you beyond reason. Understandable. Come, let's speak in private so I can assuage your concerns."

Krenil took me by the arm and guided me along the Hall of Order toward his quarters.

"Good work, Loa'h," he said to a young mermaid as he swam past, "but watch the curlicue at the bottom of your inscription. It emphasizes the spirit of the law."

We left the Hall of Order and traveled through several more nondescript, white passages. He led me into his entry chamber and lit several luma crystals. The room was otherwise empty.

"Now, what's this all about?"

"You gifted me a trident you knew was useless, didn't you? I also think you rigged Ariella's chip to get her sacrificed!"

Krenil put his hand to his chest. "Why would I do that? You know I love Ariella. I've offered to absolve her."

"Only if she marries you."

"True. Rules do need to be followed. Have we an answer from Ariella?"

"She said no!"

"She refused?" Krenil cocked his head to the side, eyes narrowed.

"Of course, she did. She doesn't want anything to do with you. She told me she'd rather be sacrificed."

Krenil tapped his trident against the luma crystals. The room went dark.

"What are you doing?"

A shrill whistle sounded. Moments later, something hit me in the face. Strong hands wrested my trident away and pinned my arms behind my back.

"Let me go!" I shouted as I struggled. Whoever grabbed me was strong. Without a weapon, I was no match.

They dragged me into the corridor. Two soldiers held me.

"I am Regent!" I shouted.

"Even the Regent is not immune to certain laws." Krenil stroked his beard as he swam beside us. "You committed treason against the Tentacle Lord. You just admitted that you spoke with the sacrificial victim and neither tried to apprehend nor brought her to us."

"You offered to marry her!"

Krenil shrugged. "An offer she has not accepted. I followed the rules. You did not."

I lunged toward him but the soldiers were too strong. Something cracked in my left arm. Merrow watched with gaped mouths while the soldiers dragged me down the broad hallway.

"I'm Regent. Father pronounced me Regent!" I shouted. They did nothing. The soldiers tossed me into a cell and locked the door.

"You can't do this!"

Krenil swam away with the soldiers, then he turned back. "I know what you are, Delphin. I know why you found your initiation with Chrysalis so... difficult. Do you think you've hidden that from me all these years?"

Acid roiled in my stomach. "I don't know what you're talking about."

"Oh, you do know what I'm talking about. You've learned to cloak as you've grown older, but a zebrafish never loses his stripes. If not for me, the Regent would have executed you like Barron. You should kiss my fins. I protected you all these years, hid your secrets. I helped you find a way to avoid initiation with Chrysalis. I helped you win the tournament! Jahvo died with love and pride for you far beyond what you deserved. You aren't fit to be Regent and you know it. Now call your sister. Bring her to the pod, or endure the consequences."

* * *

Calling Ariella never crossed my mind. Now I saw that she'd been right all along. I needed to do everything possible to keep her away. Private communications were possible at short distances. The only way to communicate via long distances was to shout, to broadcast. Everyone would hear it. And if she responded? They could follow her response right to her hiding place.

I yanked and pulled at the whalebone bars until my hands were red, raw, and bleeding. Despite their age, I was no match for the strength of whalebone no matter how algae encrusted.

Black rock rose around me about twenty feet high. Dim light diffused from an ancient and malfunctioning luma crystal. It was just enough to see the piles of merrow bones collected in the corner. I'd never known a place such as this existed. A dungeon.

One day passed and then another. I lost track. Stomach cramping with hunger, I scraped a layer of grotto algae from the sides of the cavern and forced myself to eat. Bitter with the strong tastes of iodine and sulfur, it was edible but disgusting. Grotto algae was primarily used to stuff sea pillows or prevent cold currents from leaking into a drafty room. I was gagging down my third mouthful when Krenil appeared.

By his side swam massive Teomath and Finner. Teomath carried an odd prickly club with serrated edges made from barnacle shells. Finner held a strange utensil that looked like a giant lobster claw. Krenil smiled and opened the cell door. He nodded his head at Teomath and Finner. The two rushed into the room.

When the club hit the side of my head, pain flashed through my jaw and temple. A white flash of light stole my consciousness. Not for long. When the lobster claw clamped down on my pinky finger, I woke up fast. Then I screamed.

Chapter Twenty-Two - Delphin

"DELPHIN! DELPHIN!" SOMEONE called my name from a distance.

I swam through the Hall of Order. There was a dictate I needed to find but thousands wrote themselves before my eyes. Finally, I found the right location. Just as I read the dictate I needed, the voice called again, louder.

"Delphin!" My sister's voice.

I struggled through sediment but couldn't reach her. Pain wracked my body. My fingers, my head, my back, my fin. Everything felt bruised. Eventually, the pain woke me. Black stone surrounded me. I glanced at a jumble of bones in the corner. Everything that happened came swirling back. I was a prisoner, Ariella's voice just a dream.

"Oh, my poor Delphin!" Ariella again.

I wrenched my head to the left, toward the bars of my cell. My sister swam there, hand reaching through the bars, tear bubbles exploding from her eyes. Her face lit up when she saw mine. She put her hand to her mouth. "Thank god, you're alive."

For a moment, seeing her face filled me with more hope than I'd felt in ages. Then I remembered the events that led me there.

"What are you doing here?" I bolted upright, and the world wavered and shifted around me. I almost threw up. "Krenil will find you!"

"Yes. I don't care. I'll marry him if it will get you out of this place."

"No! Never. You can't. He's everything you said and worse." My fin ached as I swam toward her. I reached out to take her hand and then jerked back. My fingers were purple and swollen. It hurt too much. She winced when she saw them.

I rested my head against the cold bars. "I had a dream. It reminded me of a dictate. I can take your place. That will solve everything."

"Take my place? What do you mean?" Ariella kissed my purple fingers with soft lips

"It's a statute. It permits any merrow to take the place of another in a sacrifice to the Tentacle Lord *if* they are family members. I'll take your place. You won't need to marry Krenil or stay in hiding—unless you want to. My crime won't be relevant because I'll be gone. This solves everything."

"No! This is against *my* rules. I will not let you." She folded her arms. I knew that stubborn expression well. Her face looked as rigid as one of the statues in the forbidden palace.

"Well, we have to figure out something!"

"Yes." She took my chin in her hands. "Something to help us *both*."

It felt like our minds melded as we spent the next moonits firing back-and-forth plans and schemes. Finally, we settled on a way forward. A way that would either save us or get us killed.

Chapter Twenty-Three - Elias

NEARING THE YACHT, the craft slowed. But not all the way. With a deafening crunch, they rammed the larger, more delicate vessel. *The Wolf's* hull groaned and shrieked but they must have installed reinforcements because it didn't cause any obvious damage to *The Wolf.* Luckily for the yacht, the damage lay above the waterline.

On the deck of the yacht, three men in dark suits aimed and fired. Bullets ricocheted off the deck. Elias dropped to his belly and wormed his way behind a large metal chest. He'd be out of firing range, he hoped.

The two vessels drifted around one another. The yacht revved its engine. Meanwhile, his craft. *His? Ha.* Well, the boat he happened to be a prisoner on, reversed and blocked its passage.

Elias looked up in time to see one of Silas' men—the skinny one, Omar—shout as he got shot in the stomach. Meanwhile, more men appeared on the deck of the yacht.

"We're outnumbered!" Reht shouted.

Elias rolled to the side as *The Wolf* spun around and veered away to the sound of machine gunfire. Far away from the yacht, with night falling, they stopped.

After their failed attempt, they seemed to have forgotten Elias. Silas came and tied him to an anchor fastening. He seemed distracted and his knots were careless. While the men argued, he worked his hands back and forth. His skin burned, red and raw, but the binds loosened. Just a little more.

Silas aimed his AK-47 into the sky and shot upward in frustration as if he could kill the moon herself.

Rat tat tat tat!

"Prince Amari should have been ours! Akhbar will come, and we'll have nothing to show for our time at sea."

Pavel sat bent over Omar, who moaned on a pile of blood-soaked blankets. Silas and Reht clomped over to them.

"Can you fix him?" Silas asked.

Pavel shook his head. "He needs a hospital."

"Hospital? Do you see a hospital anywhere?"

Reht bit his lip. "We should go back, Silas."

Silas crouched down. "If we go back, will you be the one who announces our failure? That we had Prince Amari and lost him?"

Reht swallowed.

"Of course, you won't! Guess who will get blamed? Me! No, no. I will prove myself, Reht. We will find the prince and capture him. I don't care what it takes or how damn long we have to spend out here. We will not return empty-handed."

Omar continued to moan. After a long half-whispered argument that Elias couldn't overhear, Silas shouted at Pavel.

"Bring whisky! Make it fast."

Pavel ran back into the cabin and returned with a glass bottle. Silas took it and held it to Omar's lips. Omar coughed.

"Drink more," Silas said. The alcohol calmed Omar and his eyes drifted close.

"C'mon," Silas said.

When the three of them lifted Omar, he woke up and shrieked in pain. They carried him to the side and tossed him over. Elias heard a brief cry, some splashing and then nothing. He shivered despite the warmth. He was trapped with madmen, criminals—pirates of the worst sort.

Chapter Twenty-Four - Delphin

ARIELLA AND I faced Krenil and two council members. Krenil swam in the middle. Finner and Teomath floated on either side of us.

With Father dead, the council once again met in their proper chambers. Like most chambers, it was a simple white room with a white, raised table in the center.

"You were wise to return, Ariella," Krenil said with a toothy smile. "For you and your brother's sake." The sound of his voice swirled my guts with anger and shame. Anger at what he had done, shame that I'd allowed myself to be fooled. Never again would someone trick me with false kindness.

"Now, we're all here so let's get this settled. Ariella, it appears there was a misunderstanding. We were engaged. This rendered your selection as the next sacrifice void. You ran off before I could explain. Is that your understanding?"

"No. That is not my understanding," Ariella said.

"Oh? That's not your understanding? So we were not to be engaged?"

Ariella hesitated. "No," she said.

Krenil clenched his jaw and two veins I'd never noticed popped out in his forehead. "Understood. Then the sacrificial selection remains valid. Delphin's crimes also remain valid and punishable. Take Ariella to the sacrificial holding cell. Return Delphin to the dungeon to await a formal trial."

"Wait!" I said. "I, Delphin, son of Jahvo assert the following. I claim the right to take my sister's place as sacrifice."

The room went quiet.

Krenil's face went pale. "You, you…"

"Dictate 4592 section 98 states that any family member may take the place of a sacrificial victim."

The council members murmured. J'ors, a bald man with a moon face, turned to Krenil. "Is this rule inscribed?"

Krenil nodded. "Highly unusual, but yes. Inscribed it before my time. Unnecessary. It was to be amended to require council approval."

"Yet it was not amended, does not require anyone's approval, and it is therefore valid." Ariella's eyes flashed in vindication.

Krenil swallowed. "Take Delphin to the sacrificial holding cell. Ariella remains free."

* * *

The sacrificial cell was much more comfortable, except for one thing: it lay right off one of the main corridors. It was a public cell. Part of the ritual. People could come and pay their respects and give thanks to the sacrifice.

I barely got any rest. When people heard what I'd done for Ariella, I became a hero once again. Back in the dungeon, I'd subsisted on cave slime. To Krenil's displeasure, merrow brought me every delicacy. Shrimp with veins so plump and pink they made my eyes water when I ate them. Fish with flesh so delicate they practically dissolved before they reached my mouth.

Days passed, and I almost began to believe it myself. I was a hero. Niggling at the back of my mind was the plan I'd concocted with Ariella. Once enacted, I'd no longer be a hero. I'd be reviled. An exile. Weight lifted from my chest as I realized I no longer cared. There was no place for me here.

The day before the new moon, I enacted part one of the plan. I waited until many well-wishers clustered nearby. Then I made my request to Krenil and Abalon.

"Krenil." I allowed tear bubbles to float from my eyes. "I would like to see Father's death place before I am sacrificed."

"Abalon needs to use her chambers for healing." A pained, annoyed expression flashed across Krenil's face. "It's unnecessary. You can visit his memorial if you wish to mourn."

Abalon shot Krenil a surprised look. "Sir, it would be no bother for him to visit. I have no patients right now."

"I want to visit the place last touched by his spirit. There's no regulation against that, is there?" I was certain there wasn't. While we had rules for almost everything, there were an infinite number of things not covered by the labyrinth of regulations.

"No, there is not. Fine."

Krenil summoned far more guards than needed. Finner, Teomath, and four other soldiers. A crowd of jubilant supporters swam with me, touching my fin for luck as we went.

When we reached the door to the healing ward, I fell against the rock, allowing grief to overcome me. It wasn't difficult. "Abalon, can I have a moment alone, to grieve?"

"Yes, Young Master!" Abalon took my hands to her mouth and kissed them.

Krenil waved his finger in the water. "No. It's a plan to escape. You haven't fooled all of us!"

I put my hand to my heart and bowed my head as if his comment caused me a near mortal wound. The crowd grumbled with disapproval.

"Sir, there is only one entrance to this room, you needn't worry," Abalon said. "Delphin is a merman of honor. After what he's done for his sister, we owe him this one small courtesy."

The crowd affirmed me. A stinging sensation of guilt rose in my belly. Was I any different from Krenil? I pushed the thought from my mind. It was his corruption that forced me into this position.

Abalon ushered me into the room and shut the portal behind me. I rushed to her herb bed, frantic to find the plant Ariella told me about. Singing Flower, BubbleBerry, Bloodroot. I'd paid no attention to Abalon's bewildering array of sea plants. There were hundreds!

A blue flower. Ariella said to look for a small blue flower with silver seeds. Caustic in the water, deadly if taken internally. Meanwhile, the moonits passed. If Krenil or the guards entered while I foraged on the other side of the room, far from where Father passed, my whole plan might collapse.

Gently pushing aside two large purple sea fans, I found what I looked for. Hands shaking, I gathered ten silver seeds from delicate blue flowers and placed them beneath my tongue.

I swam back to the spot where Father had died and laid my forehead against it. Moonits later, the portal opened. Krenil entered with Abalon.

"You've grieved long enough," Krenil said. "Now come." Finner and Teomath swam behind him. They grabbed me on either side and led me out.

Someone in the crowd had brought a handful of anthem crystal. It was reserved for weddings but now they threw the glittering substance in the air as I was taken back to my cell. I smiled and nodded as I swam through the sparkling water, trying not to jostle the precious seeds in my mouth. Now I just had to hope they would remain intact until the sacrifice tomorrow.

Chapter Twenty-Five - Delphin

MOONITS PASSED LIKE seconds and sacrifice day arrived. The hallway was so crowded with cheering clicking merrow that it took forty soldiers to clear a passage wide enough to bring me through. My heart throbbed in my chest as I swam.

"Where's Ariella?" Krenil scanned the crowd with narrowed eyes.

I bowed my head. "She doesn't want to watch. It's too painful."

Krenil said nothing as he adjusted the ever-present knife that hung wrapped at his side. I thought of the sheath I'd found. I wondered if it was a match? If all went well, I'd find out soon enough.

A hush descended as the guards led me into the center of the Hall of Tentacles. Blood stained the white platform where others' fins had been pierced. These stains were against the rules to clean. They were a badge of dedication to our Tentacle Lord.

I wondered again what the implications were of what I was about to do. The soldiers led me to the center and tied me with a thick sea frond. Krenil approached and unsheathed his knife.

"I, Krenil, sitting Regent of the merrow tribe, hereby sacrifice you to our Tentacle Lord." He continued to babble on. Sick with anxiety, I could barely focus on the words. Next thing I knew, Krenil floated in front of me, knife in hand.

"Your sacrifice is noted, Delphin," he said, an unreadable expression on his face. Just as he was about to raise the knife, I shifted my tongue, brought the seeds beneath my teeth and ground down.

I spat the pollen out in a plume, allowing the seawater to wash my mouth, gagging but careful not to swallow. Krenil choked and gasped as the caustic material closed his throat and blinded his eyes. His grip loosened on the knife. My hand shot out. I grabbed it with only a small wound on my palm to show for it.

Soldiers rushed toward the altar. Cries of fear and confusion rose from the crowd. Before the guards reached me, I slashed the sea fronds that bound me and swam as fast as I could. My speed served me well. Although the soldiers were fast, they weren't fast enough. The crowd was too confused to help them. It had all happened quickly.

I dodged left and then right and through a grove of kelp that led to the secret passage Ariella had told me about. I slipped through just as three soldiers zoomed past, continuing their hunt in the wrong direction.

The plan had worked. Well, half the plan. The most difficult part was yet to come. For that, I needed to meet my sister at our secret location.

Chapter Twenty-Six - Delphin

I swam through a maze of abandoned passages. Broken bits of rubble littered the seafloor. In some areas, the debris was piled nearly as high as the top of the passage and I had to take care not to scrape my belly. Eventually, I arrived in a vast open space. High above me, through a break in the ceiling, light filtered down from the surface. Large green kelp fronds waved gently in the almost non-existent current.

The knife's hilt remained cold in my hand, as if it were made of sea ice. The debris cleared, and I swam through a long corridor where giant statues towered on either side. Encrusted in barnacles and seaweed, they still maintained their past glory.

Mer-warriors rode enormous white alabaster sea horses. Farther along, another statue displayed a young mermaid with a baby in her arms, the baby's lips suckling at her giant bare chest of smooth stone.

Even in the filtered light of the failing luminance, I blushed. Father told me that earlier times had been periods of immorality. That is what led them into war and strife. Now, mermaids and mermen stayed fully covered in their sea-lace garments except on Spawning Day. I'd never seen a naked body.

I quit gawking at the statues and hurried. Swimming fast through this corridor made me dizzy. The statues loomed like giants. As I swam, I had the eerie sense they might topple over and crush me. I was torn between the urge to flee and the desire to stop and inspect another fascinating detail.

Up ahead, the corridor ended and branched off into three. With a strong thrust of my fin, I pushed ahead. I was nearly at the end when I stopped. The second to last set of statues were like nothing I'd ever seen.

They reclined in an enormous half shell fashioned into a bed or perhaps an altar. Two mermen easily forty or fifty fins tall lay together. One rested his head on the other's chest, while the other's giant stone hand gently rested on the back of his head. Unlike the broken statue Barron had been buried beneath, these two were still intact. Their lower regions were covered in sea moss, but they were naked.

I swam closer, heart pounding in my chest. A powerful yearning for Elias welled up. To be that free to love! My entire body trembled. Right now, I felt more certain than ever that I was making the right choice. I swam toward my destiny. The passage coiled and spiraled deeper. As I rounded a bend, I entered familiar territory.

Ariella had led me this way the last time we'd gone into the big ocean. The time that I'd found the photo of Elias. How many moons had that been now? Only a few, and already it felt like my world had drastically changed. How much more would it change another few moons from now?

Rock walls scraped against the scales of my fin as I pushed myself through the narrow space that led to Ariella's quarters. Ariella wasn't there. At first, I thought I'd missed her, but then she entered with Uncle Nebulon. I shrank back against the wall, heart pounding, trying to still my thoughts.

"Ariella!" I transmitted to her after Uncle left.

Ariella whirled around in the water, hand to her mouth. Then she swam to me.

"You did it!" she transmitted but quietly.

I nodded.

"You're certain you want to continue with the rest of your plan?" Ariella said, lips quivering. "You might never return."

"I will come back, Ariella, I promise. I'll rescue Elias and find out what the air world looks like. He'll fall in love with me, and we'll both return as mermen."

"Oh, Delphin, you and your story shells!"

"How can you say that? It was you who helped me find stories in the first place. You sound like Father."

She tapped my chest. "Don't you say that! I still believe in stories… Well, I believe in the magic of them. My scrolls. That's where the truth lies. Stories aren't facts, Delphin."

"That's exactly right, and I believe in the magic of stories too. I owe it to Elias. I need to make up for everything I've done and haven't done in the past." I thumped my chest.

She kissed me on the cheek. "I'm proud of you, Brother. All this time, I thought I was the one with the courage."

"What's that supposed to mean?"

"You've tried to play by the rules. I understood why. Now you see that rules will get you nowhere."

The knife remained icy in my hand. Even the warm golden glow from Ariella's room did nothing to change its color. It glowed a brighter blue still, as if defying the room's comfort.

"Did you manage to get the sheath?"

Ariella nodded, solemn. She handed it to me. The knife slid into it with a sigh.

"Will you be okay here, alone?"

Ariella paused. "Yes, Uncle Nebulon is here. Plus, I have my own love affair to manage."

That was new to me. "With who?"

"The library. If love is worth dying for, so is knowledge. A heart must follow its truth or turn to bone." Ariella wrapped her arms around me and nestled her head in my shoulder. "Once you do this, there will be no return. I want you to be certain."

"He *will* love me," I said. "They aren't just stories."

Ariella's eyes lightened. "Perhaps not."

I handed her the sheath now with its blade. She shivered as the leather touched her skin.

"So cold. This is dark Lemurian magic."

"Old magic. Doesn't make it dark. Will it work without Krenil? Without the Tentacle Lord?"

Ariella bit her lip. "Yes. I think Krenil has much less power than he'd like us to believe."

I nodded, wanting to believe her.

"You'll be slower without your fin." She eyed the knife with distaste.

"True." I'd no longer be the fastest merrow in the pod. I paused for a minute, sad at the thought. Then I nodded. "I'm ready."

I leaned back, arching my spine and presented my tail, teeth gritted together. "Directly in the center. Don't hesitate. I'll try not to scream. It might be best if you left fast in case Krenil's soldiers hear."

Ariella blinked several times and swallowed. She unsheathed the blade and lifted the knife above her. Pain rippled across her brow and she hesitated. "Delphin—I don't know if I can. It's so violent."

"You have to, for me. Make it quick. Please!"

Ariella's face hardened with determination. With a sharp gasp, she brought the knife down and stabbed me. A flash of icy cold spiked through my fin and rocketed all the way up my spine into my brain.

For a moment, I saw nothing but a spinning white disc. Then the disc rotated and fell into two halves.

"Ariella, it's happening!" When I looked down, my tail was splitting apart down its middle. It didn't hurt exactly, but it left me with a horrible feeling, as if my whole body might split.

Ariella put her hand to her mouth. The knife fell to the coral below with a distant *clink*.

"Are you sure you don't want to come with me?" I grabbed her hands.

Tear bubbles popped from her eyes. "Oh, Delphin, when I listened to those story shells, I pictured being brought to dry land by a human's kiss, not a knife to my belly. My work is here with the scrolls."

She grabbed the knife, slid it back in its sheath, and handed it to me. "Take it. You might need it to protect yourself." She pressed her lips hard to mine and pushed me out of the passage. "I love you, Brother! Now swim!"

Chapter Twenty-Seven - Delphin

ALREADY, I FEARED I'd made a horrible mistake. My two human sticks...
legs, throbbed. Not only that, they were useless for swimming.
Something bumped up against me from below. Shark? I'd never
particularly feared them. They were fast but only in short bursts, and it
was easy to stay out of reach of their toothsome smiles.

It wasn't a shark. "Tango!" I cried. "What are you doing here? You
hate the open sea!" Tear bubbles crept from my eyes as I wrapped my
hand around him and sobbed as he breached the surface. I was happy
he was here. A little piece of home. However, he wouldn't be able to
travel with me where I headed.

There was one positive aspect. For the first time since I'd rescued
him, he seemed to enjoy his time in open water. He raced and darted
after a school of juicy snapper fish and caught them in his mouth.
Perhaps he no longer needed the safety of the pod? Just like me.

Tango raced ahead and around, confused about why I was so slow.
It was thanks to Tango that I had learned to swim so fast. We used to
spend hours chasing and playing. Now I might have been a starfish
creeping along the seafloor.

I tried kicking my legs together and separately. When I kicked them
together like my fin, they did almost nothing. Separate, I couldn't
manage the coordination. The stupid things were practically useless!
Never in my life had I felt more frustration toward a body part. In fact,
the legs didn't feel like they were part of me at all. I'd be lucky to beat
a flounder.

Flat blue ocean rippled around me as I cut the surface and gulped in
air. Delicious air. No longer was I a creature of water. Now I was a land
creature—too slow to survive alone in the sea. However, the boat was
gone. Elias was gone. But what I felt most was the fact that my fin was

gone.

"I hate legs!" I slapped the water. "Hate! Hate! Hate! Hate them!" I spun around in fury until I became even more exhausted. Tango rose to the surface and chattered at me. "It's not funny, Tango!"

Exhausted, I floated on my back. As I stared up at the blue sky, I started to laugh and couldn't stop.

What is the point of losing something so dear to me if now I can't even rescue Elias? What was I thinking? Even sacrifice to the Tentacle Lord might have been better.

To my right lay the island where I'd left Elias. The water had grown still. I floated confused for a moment. Earth and sky reflected in the water. I couldn't tell the difference between the two. A strong current pushed in the opposite direction. Chest heaving, I made it to the rocks, where I lay like a beached sea creature. Tango chattered from farther in the water, unable to follow.

"Be careful out in the seas!" I shouted. "I'll be back, I promise." I wasn't sure if Tango could understand the intent behind my transmission. With a cheeky flick of his snout, he darted back below the surface, off to find more fish to gobble.

I pulled myself naked onto the sand. Near to where I lay, heaving, were Elias' footprints and evidence of the scuffle that occurred when the men took him. I thought back to the photograph of Elias and his family. Humans had colorful skins. Not me.

I watched my body, waiting for a similar skin to grow but nothing happened. Aside from my pale body, the only covering was a layer of gritty pebbles and sand. I wished Elias were here. Perhaps he'd be able to tell me about the strange human skins.

How will I ever find him?

I'd never explored all the secret nooks and crannies of my pod. From what I'd learned, the sea was even more vast.

I reached into my shoulder pouch and examined the knife, nestled in its sheath. I shivered in the sun. The bright rays made my skin ache. I realized that I hadn't yet tried my new legs for anything but swimming. That had been a failure, but I'd achieve nothing by lying around all day.

Angling my right leg in front, I leaned forward and used a boulder as support. Jabs of pain shot up through the center of my feet. It felt odd to stand. The pebble beach looked very far below. A gust of wind blew, and I stepped back. My legs gave away. I tumbled into the sand onto my behind. My head throbbed. It had been painful to stand, yet exhilarating. I crawled to a large rock formation and pushed myself up again. This time, I used a larger boulder to steady myself.

It was an interesting experience… to stand. I felt a pull from the earth; she wanted to bring me back close to her. Multiple times I keeled over and fell to my knees or onto my backside. It didn't matter. I continued to practice. Over and over again, I stood and then I fell. No matter how much it hurt, I had to learn. The sun arced closer toward the ocean by the time I could walk a few steps without falling.

The pain remained and I was clumsy but I'd made progress. I sat down in the shade of an overhanging boulder and wiped sweat from my brow. I'd had no idea it was such hard work to be human. Poor Elias. I allowed my eyes to close and nearly dozed off when I spotted something. More footprints.

When the men came and captured Elias, I'd seen one of them walk deeper onto the island. Even though it had now been several days, I noticed the disturbance the man's feet left. I stood. Without falling! Then I followed the footsteps until they ended farther down the shore.

I continued along the beach and only fell twice. Night would come soon and I wanted to find a safe place to rest. Perhaps there would also be some food, hopefully, fish.

Beyond the rocky shore were a cluster of strange spiky-leaved plants huddled around a pool of water. It seemed to be a natural reservoir, although the water wasn't salty. A rocky path led up a steep ridge to the spot where I'd seen Elias signal for help. I followed the trail.

The view was stunning. It made me so dizzy that I stumbled and fell down. When my knees contacted the hard-packed dirt and stone, the jolt shook my bones. The air world was a hard and unforgiving place. I'd need to be careful.

When I reached the clifftop, I lay back on the ground catching my breath and stared up at the sky. So blue, cold, and impassive. Looking at it for too long made me queasy, I turned to look at the comforting browns and greens that reminded me of the seaweeds from home. An odd woven series of branches caught my eye.

Crawling over, I pulled on it with my fingers. It was a door made to look like plants and vines. I gave it a hard yank, and it fell forward, revealing a dark opening.

It wasn't a large cave. It was crammed full of human objects that dwarfed anything I'd ever found in Ariella's secret spot. They were all in pristine condition. The ocean hadn't eaten these items.

There were several large metal boxes I couldn't open. One of the wooden containers I managed to break open with a stick. It contained those horrible gray, metal objects. Guns. Many guns. Long ones and short ones. I held one in my hand. It felt cold… and dangerous.

The cave was filled with weapons. Guns and also knives. Outside, the light faded. Soon it would be dark. I'd sleep here. First I had to eat though if I wanted to maintain my energy. Even with my legs, I should be able to catch a fish or two.

I walked outside, thankful that the sun was less intense. My skin had reddened and blistered, not accustomed to sun exposure. Back at the spot I'd landed, I slurped water from the cupolas hidden in rocks farther from the water. It was just enough to make me even more thirsty. My new land body needed water. Instincts I'd never experienced before awakened. I walked back and drank from the larger pool of water I'd found.

After a good long drink, my belly grumbled. Nothing was straightforward! Back home, food was plentiful and easy to come by. Being the son of the Regent, food was made for me at each of our four daily mealtimes. Here I'd need to fend for myself.

Several fins-length from shore, I spotted a school of sunfish. I swam out and jabbed my knife toward them. My aim was off. I was too tired. They scattered. I wished I'd been able to bring my trident. I ate a few small clams sunk deep into the sand. Their flesh had never tasted so delicious.

Back on the beach, I lay against the rock, bare skin against stone in the same shaded area Elias had sat. Even though he was gone, it comforted me to be in the same place. The sun fell into the ocean—a giant eye of fire. Air and sky were so big, it overwhelmed me, yet my eyes could not stop drinking it. My eyes closed. Time to sleep.

I trudged back toward the cave. Motion out of the corner of my eye startled me. Something hit me hard on the side of the head. I crumpled to the hard ground.

Chapter Twenty-Eight - Elias

ELIAS WOKE TO the sound of men shouting on deck. He felt dazed. Last night, the ocean had been dead calm and the heat stifling. Air snuck down a single two-inch diameter ventilation tube that led up to a covered part of the deck. It wasn't enough.

Deep in the night, he'd stood sweating with his mouth pressed to the tube's hole. No matter how hard he inhaled, he couldn't get enough oxygen. After a while, he'd given up and fallen into delirious sleep.

Stretching, he rolled his aching neck first to the left and then the right, trying to ease the kinks out. He pulled his dirty t-shirt over his head. With nothing in the hold except for crates of tinned goods, he'd balled it up and used it as a makeshift pillow on the metal floor.

Beneath the ventilation tube, he stood on his tiptoes, trying to hear what was happening above. If he put his eye in just the right spot, a tiny part of the deck was visible when the boat rolled in a swell.

Elias walked to the hatch. He yanked and tugged on the handle for the hundredth time. He'd kept his escape attempts low key. It wouldn't do much good to escape from the cell in the middle of the sea. Even Timu, an experienced fighter, wouldn't have been able to take over the boat by himself. Well, Timu would probably say otherwise. Elias smiled in the dim light.

With a loud clang, the hold door exploded open and banged against the metal wall. Elias stumbled backward, landing hard on his elbow.

"Who the hell is he?" Silas yelled.

Without giving Elias a chance to answer, Silas came and wrenched Elias' throbbing arm behind his back. Silas forced him up the precarious ladder to the deck. He pushed him hard and he fell, slamming his forehead against the metal deck. The tangy iron-rich taste of fresh blood filled his mouth. Disoriented, Elias lay blinking in the intense sun.

Despite his throbbing head, it felt good to breathe fresh air and feel sunlight on his face. As his eyes adjusted, he saw Silas, Reht, and the older one, Pavel, standing around a body tied and bound on the deck.

"Well?" Silas asked.

Elias looked down at the naked youth on the deck and his heart skipped a beat. That face. It had been from a distance but he was sure it was the mysterious figure he'd seen out in the water. He had the fine features of a model. Even the way he lay, he looked like he'd been arranged for a magazine photoshoot.

"He knows him," Silas said. "They're working together."

"No, that's not true." Elias shook his head.

"Liar. You know him." Silas turned to Pavel. "Can I read a face? You ever lie to me, Pavel?"

Pavel shook his head as he puffed a long stream of smoke from his lips. "Never, boss. Wouldn't dare."

"Why not?"

"Cause you'd always know."

Silas nodded. "Damn right I would, dickwad. Reht, wake him up!"

Reht shook the youth. He groaned. Silas took the cigarette out of his mouth and put it out against the kid's hand. The boy's eyes flew open, and he screamed. Those eyes. Violet-blue. It had been from a great distance, but Elias would never forget them.

"What's your name?" Silas squatted in front of the kid. He was about the same age as Elias. Sixteen or seventeen. He stared up at Silas, dazed.

"How hard did you hit him?" Silas muttered. "I didn't say bash his brains out. We need to figure out where these two came from."

"I told you. I'm a refugee," Elias said. "Maybe he is too."

"Shut up! I'm not talking to you. Refugees don't carry pretty knives like these!" Silas gestured to an object Reht turned over in his hand.

Elias' eyes widened. The last time he'd seen the sheath, it had fallen into the ocean. How had they found it? It hadn't held a knife. Ever. Now it did.

"That's—" *Mine*, Elias almost said before he stopped himself. It was his grandfather's sheath. He'd recognize it anywhere. The subtle carved symbols, and the nick on the side. Seeing it, he heard his father's voice.

Oh, yes, your great-grandfather was a warrior. It runs in the family. See this nick on the sheath? He might have died right then but oh, he was fast. He got the knife out and slit his attacker's throat.

Silas narrowed his eyes and nodded at Reht and Pavel. He turned to Elias and was about to say something more when a noise stopped him. The kid on the deck whimpered with the sound a puppy might make and opened his mouth.

Silas leaned closer. "What the hell?" He reached his fingers out and roughly forced the boy's mouth open. Instead of regular teeth, his front teeth were razor-sharp, as were his bottom teeth. Silas yanked his fingers out and swore.

"Bastard bit me!" Blood dripped from his pointer finger.

"What's with his teeth?" Pavel asked.

"Torture. Someone filed his teeth down. Punishment. I've heard of it before," Reht said. "Never seen someone with so many though. Usually, they get all broken up."

"What else you got, kid?" The boy's right fist was clenched tightly around a small object hanging from his chest. "Show it to me!"

The guy's violet eyes glowed with stubborn fire. Whoever the kid was, he had some fight in him.

Silas raised his boot and stomped down on the kid's forearm with all his weight. Crying out in pain, he opened his hand. Elias expected something valuable. It was just a cheap bone pendant on a ratty string. Reht and Silas looked down at it, disappointed.

The youth's eyes roved wildly over his captors and then to Elias. Their eyes locked, and the kid smiled as if they shared some kind of secret. Despite his odd teeth, he had a charming smile. Elias felt his heart fill with tenderness. He shoved the sudden feeling away. He didn't even know this strange kid.

"See?" Silas rubbed his temples. "They know each other." He stopped and turned to Elias. "Now we need to figure out how they found our island. And who sent 'em? Tie this one up. I don't trust either of 'em."

"No one sent me!" Elias said. "I swear."

Reht rolled the boy onto his belly and tied his arms around his back. Then he sat him up against the deck rail.

Silas wound up and punched Elias hard in the stomach. He bent over, heaving.

"Didn't tell you to speak," Silas growled.

Without warning, the boy threw off Reht, leapt up, and attacked Silas.

Chapter Twenty-Nine - Delphin

PAIN SEARED THE palm of my hand. A horrible smell filled my nose. They'd hurt me with fire. I'd heard of it in a story shell, although I'd never experienced it firsthand.

My eyes fluttered open. Several men stood above me making noises… speaking. It took me a bit of time to figure out what they were saying. It was a human language. Already my mind began to decode the sounds and make meaning where there had been none. I linked some words to anger, others fear. Mainly anger. These men wanted something. I was not sure what.

These men are bad.

I scowled up at my captors. The brilliant sun hurt my eyes and my skin stung from the sun I'd taken the day prior. Life beneath the surface felt insulated and calm compared to the raw experiences here. No matter where I turned, it seemed brutality waited.

I mustered the most intense burst of sonar possible at the man's head. The man squinted and rubbed his temples. Other than that, nothing happened. My stomach fell. Sonar at that level could disable a bull shark and even larger attackers. Here on land, it seemed useless. I wiggled my fingers, testing the strength of the rope that bound my limbs.

One man stood aside and I saw Elias. A glimmer of relief filled my belly. Although he looked tired and smelled dehydrated, he was alive! Even more handsome than I remembered, he stood, with his arms tied behind him. There was more discussion.

Fingers jammed into my mouth, pulled back my lips. The man's fingers had an unpleasant taste, sour and bitter. I bit. Not hard but enough to get the message across. *Get your stinking fingers out of my mouth.*

The man roared. When he touched me, I picked up his name. *Silas. His name is Silas.* Silas stood and stomped over to Elias, shouting.

Elias shook his head and responded.

Silas drew his elbow backward and punched Elias hard in the gut. I gasped and felt a sharp pain in my stomach.

Hot rage filled my head. My arms were knotted behind me, feet bound. It didn't matter. With a guttural cry, I wrenched my muscles hard as I could and stood. Lunging forward, I used the only weapon available. The teeth they seemed fascinated by.

I fell face-first into Silas' shoulder and bit down. Silas screamed. He turned and smashed me with his fist and I fell back to the hard surface. My ears rang and a wave of nausea washed over me. As I fell back to the deck, I glimpsed the sea. Small waves hid him, but I caught the glimpse of a fin. Tango swam around the boat. He must have followed.

Tango. Maybe he could help? A glimmer of hope shot through me. I transmitted simple images to him as hard as I could just before I got thrown back down.

Blood drenched Silas' shirt. Hands pinned me to the deck. A blunt object struck me in the temple, once, twice, three times. What help would my pet dolphin be in a situation like this? *No help.* I realized. No help at all. I fell into unconsciousness.

Chapter Thirty - Ariella

ARIELLA WATCHED AS Uncle Nebulon pressed his lips to a large rock near an entrance to their hiding place. It looked strange. As if he kissed the stone. She snickered. He glared and began to sing. Well, not singing —more like tones. Vibration zinged up through Ariella's toes and made her head buzz.

"Uncle—" Ariella started.

Uncle motioned for her to be silent. "Do you hear that?" He closed his eyes.

Ariella listened but heard nothing.

"The sound of fins cutting through water. Several mermen. Soldiers. Hear their tridents? They're sending out more to look for us."

"I've done nothing wrong!" Ariella hissed. "Delphin sacrificed himself for me."

"He escaped! Do you think Krenil will allow that? What about me?" Uncle whispered. "I'm a wanted man!"

Ariella shrugged. "Krenil is angry but it will pass. They've tried to find us before and failed. Anyway, Uncle, you can't hide forever."

"Who says I can't? I'm happy here. Or I was happy until you and your brother came and messed everything up."

"Well, I'm sorry if I ruined your peaceful existence. Delphin and I are just trying to survive too. I never asked you to help."

His face softened. "I know that. It's the legacy of your father, Jahvo. It's all of them. They can all go to the bloody fish-pit for all I care. They've *never* sent out this many soldiers day-after-day even when they hunted for you. It's that damn knife Krenil wants. He won't rest until he finds it. I need you to get it back from Delphin."'

After Father died and Krenil took over, everything changed. Ariella caught glimpses of new sacrifices being chosen as she swam, hidden in the back passages. How would they be sacrificed without the Lemurian knife? Ariella wasn't sure. Strange things were afoot. The pod was changing in ways Ariella couldn't define. It was as if it was being poisoned from within. Krenil might destroy what was left of the merrow if she didn't take action.

"Uncle, Delphin is gone." Ariella forced away the sadness that welled up behind her eyes.

Uncle Nebulon leaned against a pile of debris. "Why did you let him take the knife?"

"He needed a way to defend himself. Plus, it might keep Krenil from making sacrifices!"

"Perhaps. But at what cost? We need more time." He rubbed his eyes. "I'm exhausted. I can't manage another ward."

"Teach me." Ariella grabbed his arm. "I should learn this. I won't let Krenil win. Never. I won't let him get us. I will remove him from power."

Uncle Nebulon nodded. "I'd best teach you to rebuild the wards. I hope you enjoy kissing stones."

Chapter Thirty-One - Delphin

A DISTANT PART of myself registered being tossed into a dark, hot room with metal floors. Elias lay slouched in the corner. I limped over to him. He slept or was unconscious. Another wave of nausea washed over me.

"I'm sorry." My head fell to his bare chest, damp with sweat. When my head touched his skin, a powerful wash of his memories flooded me. I tried to pull back but got taken with them.

"It's okay," he whispered, voice ragged. He put his arm around me.

Images flooded my mind. Elias dreamt of his ill-fated voyage. I watched as Elias gave his mother his ration of water and comforted his sister. Intense noonday sun beat down on a boat. No land in sight. No ships. Nothing but heat. Heat and death.

Chapter Thirty-Two - Elias

ELIAS STIRRED IN restless sleep. He dreamed of his mother. He dreamed of his sister. He dreamed of the horrible events that happened on the boat before they sunk.

On the second day, the old man died. Their boat's captain, if you could call him that, blamed it on natural causes.

The captain searched the dead guy's pockets for kratom one more time before they whispered a quick prayer and slid his body off the plank into the ocean. They were at the captain's mercy. Elias tried to to stay rational and calm. What choice did he have?

The captain stuck his finger to the wind, murmured something to himself and pulled the rudder in the opposite direction. The engine groaned and chortled and they headed off again.

Enough was enough. "Circles," Elias whispered to Nijah. "We're traveling in damn circles." He stumbled over the maze of limbs and belongings that littered the bottom of the boat.

Battered suitcases, wicker crates, old cardboard boxes. Everyone brought what they could carry. Elias brought the backpack Timu had given him for his fifteenth birthday. A military brand, sleek blue and beige. He took such good care of it that it looked like new. It stood out amongst the ragged canvas sacks and worn chickpea bags of the others.

When Elias reached the captain, he tapped him on the shoulder. The man turned, eyes red, lips trembling. Kratom withdrawal. Perhaps other substances too. Now the transaction Elias observed as they departed made sense. Their broker, the man who'd sold them this ride to safety and freedom, had paid their captain in drugs. Now he'd run out.

"What are you doing?" Elias asked. He tried to keep the anger from his voice but wasn't successful.

"Huh? What's the problem?" the man asked, licking dry lips.

"We're practically out of water. We had barely enough food for two days. You're navigating us in circles!" Elias shouted, unable to hold back.

Two men behind him mumbled in agreement. Most on the boat were middle-aged or older. All except Nijah and him. The hot weather and lack of water and food had sapped the others of their will.

In the first hours after they left port, Elias grew sick of their complaints. The seats were too hard, one got seasick. Now that he needed them to have his back, they sat gaping, eyes bugging as if they couldn't believe the circumstances that had befallen them.

"I was deceived!" the captain snarled. "I wanna get off this boat as bad as you. But the rudder sticks, the compass is jammed on east."

"You noticed none of that until now?" Elias said. "No. You didn't care because you got your drugs and the rest didn't matter." Lightning flashed in the distance.

"Go bugger yourself and sit down, boy." The captain jutted his chin toward Elias and snapped his fingers toward the seats.

Elias came from the desert. He'd have been the first to admit that he didn't have an extensive knowledge of boats or navigation. However, one summer, before the war broke out, he'd helped his uncle on his fishing boat.

He'd learned the basics. How to read a nautical map and navigate using dead reckoning. That type of navigation depended on basic, working equipment. This fool knew nothing and there were no proper instruments.

Elias pushed him aside and grabbed the rudder. "I won't sit and let you run us in circles. You're heading us straight into a storm. We can at least try to outmaneuver it."

Finally, Elias received support from those behind him. From his sister, first. "We need food and my mother needs water! She's sick. Listen to him. There's no pride in this. I've watched you shake and shiver all morning. Go lay down and rest before you hurt us all."

And then a man came from behind and yanked at the captain. Or so-called captain.

"Liam! The boy's right," the man said.

The man forced Liam back. That was good because Liam's fists had clenched and his whole body shuddered. Luckily, his brain being as drug-addled as it was, by the time he might have caused trouble, the man had him sitting down.

Elias considered suggesting they tie Liam up, but it seemed they had him under control. He turned the boat and increased the engine's throttle. The gas gauge stated *Full*, which was impossible since they'd been running for over a day now.

Elias had no idea how much petrol they had left. It was true, the compass did not work. The man who sold them seats on this boat might very well have sent them to their deaths. Only luck would see them off this craft.

There was no way he'd be able to navigate to Europe. He didn't know how to navigate by the stars or have any idea what their final coordinates were. Soon he saw that there was no way he was going to outrun the storm. He only wasted precious petrol trying. But if he cut the motor, they'd be in real trouble. He had to keep them oriented or they might capsize.

"Now who's driving us in circles!" Liam cackled from his prone position. Elias ignored him, focusing on keeping the craft's bow oriented toward the giant waves that lifted them up and down deep, black troughs. Wind and salt flayed the air as black clouds sliced blue sky. Waves breached the side. They rode too low in the water.

"Throw it over! Throw it all over!" one of the old men shouted. Elias watched as the men began tossing over their precious belongings. Nijah wept as she threw over the tiny wooden box she'd brought—a gift from their grandmother.

He regretted losing their belongings, especially his grandfather's knife sheath and the few photos they'd brought. The rudder jerked in his hand and he turned back to the raging ocean. With a boat this small in a storm this large, it didn't make much difference whether there was someone at the controls. Yet, to stand away would have felt like giving up.

When Elias glanced back, Nijah huddled against Inas, head in her hands. With the wet and the wind tearing at them, Elias worried they'd be snatched into the deluge.

He never learned what happened next. There was a loud crack, and Elias felt an intense pain in the back of his head. Perhaps Liam attacked him from behind in a drug-addled rage? Or maybe he fell backward amid a rogue wave and slammed his head? When he opened his eyes, the boat was sinking. He flailed at the surface, half-conscious.

"Mom! Nijah!" he shouted. Nothing came out but a salty croak.

Another wave hit. Bubbles surrounded him as the force of the water pummeled him beneath the sea. Something grabbed at him. When he opened his eyes, a youth his age swam in front of him. A boy with a fin!

The boy touched Elias' chest. Elias' terror disappeared, replaced by a heavy blanket of peace. When he opened his eyes, the boat was gone, the boy was gone, Nijah and Mother were gone. Elias lay on a small, rocky island.

Chapter Thirty-Three - Delphin

ELIAS. I TRIED to say the word, but it came out an unintelligible squeak. "Elias!" Clearer but not by much. Elias' head lolled to the side, breath shallow. His arm sprawled to the side, left eye and cheek puffed out and swollen. Congealed blood caked his lips.

I stroked back his hair. I couldn't wipe the images I'd seen from my mind. His poor mother, his poor sister.

I put my face in my hands and shook with sadness. Grief and regret flooded through me with relentless fury. Tsunamis of emotion had washed over me back in the pod when Barron died, but never like this. This… this was torment.

Holding my knees to my chest, I moaned and rocked. Leaning over, I put my forehead against the cool metal of the boat's hull. Just a whisper of the sea came through. Not enough to calm me. Right now, I would have given anything to swim. To feel saltwater's comforting embrace. Or better yet, to see Ariella.

Elias? I transmitted. Did that work here? My feet and legs ached and burned with a strange fire. For a moment, I couldn't breathe. The air choked me.

Am I dying?

I thumped my head against the metal hull, softly at first but then harder. With each bang, a bolt of pain shot through my head. A flash of light… and then buzzing darkness. As much as it hurt, it was better than the emotional pain attacking me from every direction.

The rhythm soothed me. Like a heartbeat. The more my head hurt, the less the horrible truth of what I'd seen affected me. Suddenly, a hand yanked my shoulder.

"What the hell are you doing?" Elias shouted. He pushed me away from the wall. "Are you some kind of mental case?" His voice was slurred from his swollen lip.

Elias! I transmitted and threw my arms around him.

Elias patted me on the shoulder. "Hey, man, it's okay. Just chill out, all right?"

I leaned back and looked at Elias' face, handsome even in its wounded state.

"So do you talk?" Elias asked.

Yes! Can you hear me?

Elias cracked a bemused smile and waved his hand in front of my face.

"Hello? Where are you from?"

Elias couldn't hear my transmissions. He disentangled himself from my embrace. I clutched his hand. I didn't want to lose our link. Maybe with enough force, I could transmit to him so he could understand? Speaking was so difficult.

I come from the sea. What happened to you was the fault of my people. The merrow. I stared deep into Elias' eyes.

"Hey." Elias shook my shoulder. "I just asked you a question."

My transmissions were not working.

"I... Delphin." I pointed to my chest.

"You're a dolphin?" Elias massaged his head. "My brain hurts too much for games."

I thought of Tango and laughed. I shook my head. "Not dolphin. Delphin. My name."

"You sound like a dolphin. What did they do to your voice?"

"Just need... practice." My voice was getting much stronger.

"Okay..."

"Can you understand me now?"

Elias nodded and removed my hand from his and eased himself down by the wall. He closed his eyes. "We should have never left Farad."

I sat next to him, shoulder-to-shoulder, thigh-to-thigh. Elias shifted a few inches away and gave me an odd look. It puzzled me. I could tell that Elias wanted me close, that it felt good for him too. Yet he resisted.

"If Barron were here, he'd get us out of here. He'd kill them all!"

Elias nodded. "If Timu was here, he'd blow their heads off." Elias paused. "Who's Barron?"

"He was... a good friend," I answered. "Who's Timu?"

"Same."

Suddenly, there was a loud *bang* and light filled the room. Two shadowy figures loomed in the doorway.

"Back!" a thundering voice commanded.

They pushed us against the wall. Silas kicked an empty tin plate across the room.

"If you think we'll feed you buggers much longer, you're wrong. Now tell me. Who. Sent. You. Here?" he shouted. "And why?"

Elias folded his arms. "I already told you."

"Shut the hell up! You." He pointed at me. "Who sent you?"

"No one sent me."

Silas' lips curled up in contempt. He kicked the tin cup against the wall and it hit inches from my head. I winced.

He took several steps forward. "Tomorrow. Dawn. Either I get the answers I need or I'll put bullets in your brains and feed you to the fish."

My heart pounded in my chest as Silas turned and left. I smelled Elias' fear trickle beneath his arms. I'd done enough harm. Somehow, I had to get us to safety.

Chapter Thirty-Four - Ariella

THE CORRIDOR OPENED into an orb-shaped space covered in purple amethyst veined with blue lapis. Ariella paused and gazed around, amazed. No sea floss had gathered in this room. Had someone cleaned it? The room extended forty or fifty feet above her and about the same below.

Floating in the middle gave her the sensation of dangling in the heart of an immense jewel. She'd lost herself in the experience when motion down the passage to her left stopped her reverie.

Sending out her awareness, she confirmed her instinct. Whatever approached her moved fast, and it was not merrow. It was a sea animal.

Father warned them that ancient predators had taken over the forbidden areas. Uncle Nebulon convinced her those were just stories to scare off curious merrow. Now she feared Father had been right. If only she had a trident! Ariella searched the room for a weapon. Swimming to a wall, she tugged at a large chunk of amethyst, but it lay embedded in the structure.

Pulling herself as close to the wall as possible, she waited. Seconds later, the animal burst out of a corridor on the far end. And it was... Tango? She sent out a soft transmission, and Tango stopped swimming and circled toward her.

"I wondered what happened to you!" Ariella stroked the animal. Tango looked healthier than when she'd seen him last, and his skin disorder had healed. It seemed the open ocean treated him well. Maybe he'd been stealing too much food from the kitchen?

"You must miss Delphin as much as I do," Ariella whispered as he chattered. "What are you trying to tell me?" She put her hand against Tango's flank. She caught flashes of images. Delphin with legs. An

120

island. Trouble on a boat? *Danger.* Tango raced off.

"Tango! Wait!"

She couldn't keep up. Just when she'd be at the point where she might grab him, he'd give a burst of speed and dart ahead. Ariella considered sending out a burst of sonar to stun him. But she worried it would hurt him, and besides, it might alert the guards to her location. There was no choice but to follow.

Tango dashed and darted and a few times, she wondered if they went in circles. In fact, Ariella was sure they *had* gone in circles a few times. That was dolphins for you.

She followed Tango up a passage that grew wider and brighter and brighter until they reached an opening she'd never seen before. It led to the Great Sea. Ariella gave a sharp intake of water and slammed her fin down, stopping where she swam. She'd never been to the Great Sea.

Tango spun around, mouth open, as he let loose a deafening series of squeaks and screeches.

"We'll go find him, but I need Uncle's help. C'mon, Tango. Come back with me."

The dolphin swam off into the deep blue.

"Tango!"

It was too late; he was gone. Ariella spun around and swam as fast as she could back into the abandoned corridors that she'd made her home.

* * *

"Follow a dolphin into the sea? Are you mad, girl? Never. We're safest here."

"Delphin is in trouble!"

"He *is* trouble. What did you think would happen when he went chasing after a human boy? Mourn him, Ariella. Best think of him as dead. He might as well be."

"He's my brother. Your nephew! I won't just let him die out there."

"Assuming you follow his dolphin and find him, how will you help him? Bring him back here? He has legs! He's doomed himself."

"You told me there's a way to reverse it."

"Indeed. With a hefty price. Let it go, child."

Ariella shook her long tresses. "If you won't go with me, I'll find him on my own. If I had a trident—"

Uncle Nebulon's eyes narrowed. "No."

"You told me that rules and regulations don't apply here. You let Delphin use your trident. Is it because I'm female?"

"I let Delphin try it to prove a point! In the old times, mermaids and merman fought alongside one another. One day, we will return to those times, Ariella, I promise you. When the time is right, you shall have a trident if you wish. You might even rule the entire pod! But I won't support my niece in risking her life for nothing."

"For nothing? You won't help Delphin because of Barron, isn't it? You blame him for Barron's death."

Uncle Nebulon's face twisted. "Don't bring Barron into this. It has nothing to do with him."

"Well, then help me!"

Uncle's voice softened. "Trust me. Bury your mind in research as I have. That's where we'll do the most good for ourselves and for merrowkind. With Krenil in charge, we have little time before our situation becomes dire. We must remove him from power at all costs."

Chapter Thirty-Five - Delphin

ELIAS PRIED A piece of loose metal off of the bottom of the door hatch. He jiggled it back-and-forth in the lock. "C'mon, c'mon," he whispered. It snapped in his fingers and he cut his thumb.

"Damnit!" He threw the broken piece to the side and put his face in his hands. "We'll die here!"

"No." I put my hand on his shoulder. "It's okay. I have a plan."

"How can it be okay? You were banging your head against the hull last night! Now you're telling me it's okay? We're done!"

Remembering my emotional meltdown, shame flooded my gut. Being away from the water was more difficult than I imagined. While I was never known for my even temperament, being in the open air made my emotions more unpredictable than ever.

"Where did you find it?" Elias asked. "The sheath?"

I didn't understand the word. I reached out and touched his hand to access more of his language. That made it clear. It was the knife sheath he asked about.

"We found it, my sister and I."

"Where?"

"At the bottom of the sea."

A skeptical look creased his forehead.

"It was my grandfather's. We threw it overboard just before we sank." He looked at me thoughtfully. "Was it *you* who saved my life?"

I swallowed and nodded shyly, wondering how much he remembered.

"Your eyes looked familiar. I thought I dreamt the whole thing. You had a... tail?"

I smiled and shrugged.

"Well, I must have hallucinated that part." He put his hand on my shoulder. "Thank you." He leaned back and looked me in the eyes. "Did you see what happened to the others? There was a woman about thirty-five and my sister, two years younger than me. She had a bright green t-shirt."

I shook my head and closed my eyes as if that could stop the memories. "I didn't see them." I honestly hadn't. I could imagine what happened to them but didn't know for sure.

"If I survived, maybe they did too? So, what's your plan?"

"I sent a message with Tango, my dolphin. My uncle and sister will come to help us."

"A message to a dolphin?"

"Yes. Tango will transmit it to my sister and uncle—at least I hope."

"Your dolphin?" Elias slumped forward and rubbed his eyes with his left hand. "Were you pretending not to know how to speak?"

"I've learned from you."

"From me?" Elias raised an eyebrow. I found it sexy. It wasn't a facial gesture I'd seen anyone in my pod make. I tried to raise my eyebrow but couldn't raise one at a time. Instead, I raised both and dropped them. Raised them again. Dropped them. It wasn't working.

Elias blew a long sigh of air between his lips. "You're a strange guy, Delphin. So you sent a message. Okay. So, how did you end up on the island? Are you some kind of refugee or…?"

"I came to the island to help you. I had to leave my pod."

"Okay, okay. You don't have to tell me."

I stepped forward and put my hand on Elias' muscular chest. His heart beat wildly beneath my palm. I felt a brief surge of attraction from Elias but he squelched the impulse.

I lowered my hand. "You're very handsome."

Elias' face turned red and he leaned away. "I don't see what that has to do with anything."

"Back in my pod, there's an area we aren't allowed to visit."

"Where is this pod?" He folded his arms.

"Beneath the sea. To the west."

His skeptical frown deepened. "Okay."

"There are many statues there. Each one shows a different part of life, a long time ago. One of my favorites are two men in each other's arms. They loved each other. And were free to do so. Now love between two mermen or two mermaids is forbidden. I hoped here, it might be different. I want you to come back with me. When I'm Regent, I'll change the rules."

Elias sat and rested his back against the hull, closing his eyes. "Things are the same everywhere. Total shit."

"What are the rules here?" I asked.

"Stay alive? There are no rules."

I put my hand on his shoulder. He turned to me and we sat inches apart. I leaned in and tried to kiss him. He jerked his face away, scowling. "What the hell, man?"

"Who is Timu? You loved him."

Elias gaped at me, stunned. He put his hands to his temples and then looked at me again. "No one knows that. No one was ever supposed to know." His lip trembled.

"You sent it to me just now."

"I did not. Did I say his name in my sleep?" He blushed.

"I read it from your mind when I touched you."

"C'mon—" He went to stand, but I stopped him. I brought him closer and rested my forehead against his shoulder. "Please," I said.

"Timu is handsome, but not so handsome as you. He has a scar. Right here." I pointed to my lip.

"You must know him somehow. You're lying to me."

"No!" I grabbed his hands, closed my eyes, and concentrated. "The shed was dark. There was this substance everywhere that you call sand. Between your toes, in your clothes and hair. This dust everywhere. Timu touched your chest right here—" I put a gentle finger on his nipple. "Then here—" I moved my hand down to Elias' stomach. "Then here." I moved my hand lower and felt Elias stir.

His breathing grew heavier, and he pushed my hand away. "Okay, I believe you." His body trembled.

"I didn't mean to scare you. I just want you to trust me."

"What else do you know about me?"

"Nothing. I only went into your language place so I could speak to you. I didn't snoop around. Don't worry." This was a partial truth. I'd picked up bits and pieces, I'd seen his dreams while he slept. Not on purpose.

"You know a secret I've told no one in my entire life. I know nothing about you except your crazy stories." Elias grabbed my shoulders. "You need to use this talent, skill, trick, whatever it is on them. Learn their weaknesses, anything we can use to our advantage!"

"I'll try. I won't let anyone harm you, Elias, I swear. I won't let what happened to Barron happened to you. I promise!"

"Calm down. Who's Barron?"

"I killed him."

Elias went silent. He regarded me with solemn brown-green eyes. Everything that happened poured out.

"Barron was like an older brother to me. But also more. I had confusing thoughts about him. Forbidden feelings."

Elias nodded as if he understood.

"I longed for him when we were apart. My heart glowed with happiness whenever I swam beside him. The touch of his strong hands made my body flow with red hot fire!"

Elias gave a lopsided smile as if he understood. "You're an intense guy."

"I fantasized many forbidden things. Things you couldn't imagine."

"No, I can imagine stuff that would make you blush." He laughed.

"Well, one day, these fantasies… overflowed and broke through my attempt to cloak them. Barron and I were sparring. We wrestled the way young mermen do. Preparing for hand-to-hand combat. He'd grabbed me from behind, my arms pinned up behind me, his body pressed hard against mine. He was so strong."

"Was he handsome?" Elias asked.

"Very." My throat clicked. "Barron commanded me to yield. It hurt but not too much. *'Yield!'* he shouted as he applied more pressure. It hurt, but I didn't want him to stop. It felt amazing to have his strong body pressed against mine."

I closed my eyes, remembering.

"I wanted to yield, true. But to him. My cloaking failed. The fruits of my fantasies popped out and displayed themselves to him. Barron broke away. *'Stuff like that will get you killed!'* Barron said. He warned me to control myself."

Elias watched me with rapt attention. I didn't sense any judgment from him, only a keen interest and understanding. "What happened then?"

"Well, I turned away and hid. I've never felt more humiliated. Barron waited for me to calm down and then he swam to me. He told me that my feelings weren't wrong but I had to keep them from the pod or I would come to harm.

"He tussled my hair. I still remember the feel of his warm, strong hand on my head. I wanted to grab it, to kiss it, to kiss him everywhere! After that, Barron avoided me. Krenil took over my tutorship. My obsession with Barron got stronger. I followed him. I needed his touch, felt like I might die without it. I stopped sleeping."

I put my face in my hands. "I can't believe I'm telling you all this."

Elias put his arm around me. "I told you quite a lot too. Even if I wasn't consensual."

When I looked up, he was smiling.

"It was by following Barron that I learned about the hidden openings that led to the forbidden areas. Even though they became Ariella's favorite place to hide, it was me who found them. I showed her first. Every second moon, Barron came to the spot near where he now lies buried. There he met someone. Another merman. I never figured out who. It was too dark. I watched them from the shadows while my chest ached, burned, and throbbed with envy."

"What did they do?"

"They kissed. They touched. They connected their bodies in ways I'd never imagined! I was so certain that my cloaking would fail, that they would notice me. They never did. They were too enthralled."

"You were jealous, I bet," Elias said.

"Yes. Watching them was the most painful, most horrible thing, yet I couldn't stop. I came and watched twice and then a third time. It made me nauseous with envy. Why hadn't Barron done those things to me? Was I unattractive to him? Was there something wrong with me? Sleep abandoned me. I stopped eating. Krenil took me to Abalon, and she found nothing wrong.

"One day, I woke from an exhausted half-slumber to find Krenil and Abalon floating beside my sea-silk bed. Fragments of fantasies about Barron lingered in my mind.

"Weak, tired, and hungry, my cloaking weakened further. They probed. This was rude, but Krenil was worried, at least I thought. They saw Barron's rendezvous point. They saw Barron's arms wrapped around the other merman. I'm not surprised. It was all I thought of over and over. By the next moon, Father had executed Barron. He died because of me."

I leaned against Elias and wept while he held me. As I drifted off to sleep against him, I noticed something strange. For the first time since Barron died, my chest had stopped hurting.

Chapter Thirty-Six - Ariella

ARIELLA SKIRTED THROUGH hidden back passages, careful not to be seen. Krenil had absolved her, fine. However, she trusted that man about as much as a shark in a grotto of fish heads. Something horrible was happening to the pod, and she needed to stay far away until she could help Delphin.

Where would she go if she were a dolphin? Ariella had already gotten as close to the pod's kitchen as she dared. While she didn't dare venture all the way inside, Tango wasn't there as best as she could tell.

She swam back toward the forbidden area where her precious scrolls awaited. Knowing that Delphin was in trouble, she couldn't rest. There was no point in trying to concentrate on her studies.

It had only been a few days since he left. She'd seen how much slower he swam with legs. How far might he have gone?

Without meaning to, Ariella swam to the area where she'd seen Tango last. He'd wanted to guide her out into the Great Sea. She swam closer to the yawning chasm that led away from safety. Tango was not around.

Sunlight filtered through the surface, high above. It didn't look dangerous, although the expanse overwhelmed her. She felt most comfortable in enclosed tunnels and cozy rooms. The boundless blue water that lay before her looked endless. Open space was foreign. It signified danger. Ariella swam a few meters out, ready to dart back at the first sign of trouble.

Nothing. There weren't even any fish. It wouldn't do any harm to continue.

Heart thudding in her ears, she swam farther. Soon the opening that led back to safety disappeared from view. Ariella sensed it there, though—like an itch that led the way she'd need to turn if she ran into any trouble. She swam farther into the boundless blue.

Chapter Thirty-Seven - Delphin

THAT NIGHT, WE fell asleep in each other's arms.

"You're softer than this damn floor, anyway," Elias said. "Might as well make us both more comfortable." He lay his head on my shoulder. Later that night, when we both were hazy with sleep, warm hands found the ragged oversized shorts Silas gave me.

His hand rested on my thigh first. Then he moved it lower. At first, I thought it was an accident. Should I move it? I did nothing. I let his warm palm lie against me, unable to stop the stirring that rose. Feeling me warm and urgent, he pressed and slid his hand beneath the waistband of my shorts. I moaned, on fire with feelings I'd never felt.

He took my hand and guided me to him. He'd undone his pants in the dark. The hunger that I'd hidden for so long seemed as potent for him as it was for me.

A current of energy released between us at the same moment and I gasped. My body pressed tight to his, I'd never felt more connected, more in tune with anyone my entire life. It confirmed my love for him.

Afterward, we lay in a sweaty mess of half-naked skin and muscle. I went to kiss him on the lips but he turned his head.

"What's wrong? Is it my strange teeth?"

"No." He shrugged. "Your teeth are cool. It's just—"

He didn't have a chance to answer further. *The Wolf* picked up speed.

We braced ourselves as we got jolted back and forth.

Seconds later, the boat turned hard and stopped, sending us tumbling into the far wall. We lay in a jumble of limbs. My ears rang, head buzzed.

"Are you okay?" Elias asked.

I nodded. I was about to speak but the sounds of loud gunshots stopped me. *Boom, boom, boom.* A shout. Men's voices shouting. Then silence.

* * *

Reht dragged us, disheveled, disoriented, and blinking onto the deck. The boat's radio crackled with distant voices. Pavel sat hunched over a screen.

Reht tied us to a bulwark at the prow. Silas pointed a gun to my head.

Reht grabbed the knife and put it to Elias' throat. "How about I slit your throat with your own knife? We're done wasting our time. Tell us how you found that island. Last chance."

Elias glared. "Get it over with and kill me then! I told you. Our boat sunk. I left Farad with my mother and sister."

"What about you?" Silas jammed the gun into my temple.

"Remove your metal weapon and I'll tell you," I said in a calm tone.

Silas laughed. "Think you're giving the orders now? Okay." He smashed me in the face with his fist. I drooped forward, gasping. He removed the gun from my head and stuck it into my sternum hard enough that I lost my breath. "Better?"

He leaned closer and sour breath hit my face. What did these men eat? Waves of unfamiliar odors assaulted my nose.

There was just enough play in the ropes that bound my wrists for me to reach out and grab his hand. He jerked back. It wasn't much contact, but I caught something. Flashes of images. He worked for another man. Someone whom he feared.

"Are you some kinda queer?" Silas said.

Reht laughed. "The kid likes you."

"Akbhar." I pulled the sound that Silas associated with the person he worked for.

Fear. For the first time, I noticed fear from Silas.

Reht's face went pale. "Mother—"

"Akhbar!" Silas lowered the gun. "Akhbar sent you?"

I didn't know the right response so I stayed silent.

"Jesus." Reht looked out into the empty, blue horizon. "He doesn't trust us."

Silas snorted. "Akhbar doesn't trust anyone. It's how he's stayed alive."

Noise crackled on the radio. "Silas, you better listen to this!" Pavel stepped out onto the deck.

Silas' eyes darted away from me. For the first time, he looked shaken.

"That fishing boat isn't far." Pavel pointed to a small gray dot on the horizon.

"Fishermen?" Silas asked. "They won't have anything of value. Do you think *that* will impress Akhbar? He wants the prince! We must get him the prince."

Pavel sighed. "True. But they sound very excited. They've found something. Whatever they found might be valuable."

Silas tugged at his beard and stared out to sea. "They won't have much protection."

Reht shrugged. "A gun or two, maybe. Nothing we can't handle. Won't hurt to check it out. We're losing light. We won't find the prince before dark, I don't think."

Silas waved toward the boat. "Fine, fine. Let's go. It'll give me a chance to think this through."

Reht turned to Silas. "What should we do with them?" He held up his gun.

Silas scratched his chin. "Throw them back into the hold for now. I haven't decided."

Chapter Thirty-Eight - Delphin

ELIAS CLIMBED THE ladder and put his ear to the portal.

"Do you hear anything?" I croaked through bruised, swollen lips. Not long after we got thrown back into the hold, we'd heard a commotion. Shouting. Gunshots. It made me nervous. Now it was morning. We were beat.

Hopping from the ladder, Elias crouched beside me. "It's quiet now. How are you feeling?" With a light gentle touch, he caressed my bruised face.

"Oww."

Without warning, the hatch flew open with a clang. Sunlight exploded in the room. I huddled on the floor, forearm thrown in front of my eyes.

"You!" Silas shouted. "C'mon." He pointed his gun toward me. I struggled to my feet.

"Not you! " He gestured to Elias. "You stay here." He pulled me up on deck, slammed the hatch, and locked it.

We'd docked near an old boat.

"Open his mouth," Silas commanded Reht. Reht stood, chest heaving, eyes wild with fright.

"He bit you last time," Reht said. "Why me?"

"Just do it," Silas said. "If he bites you, I'll blow his skull off." He cocked his gun.

Reht put his fingers in my mouth and forced it open while Silas shone his flashlight in.

"The same. They look the same as the girl creature," Silas said.

Reht removed his fingers. "He has no scales like the other."

Fire surged through my gut. *Scales*. Teeth like mine?

"It's a strange coincidence. Get the other one too. Maybe it's part of

Akhbar's test."

On deck, the evidence of violence remained. A pool of blood shone in the rising sun.

Silas led me around to the port side and my legs buckled when I saw her. Ariella. *If they had hurt her...* Tears stung my eyes, and I lurched out of Reht's grasp and dashed toward my sister. The boom of a gun going off stopped me.

Ariella moaned. She was alive.

Pavel poked and prodded. "Perhaps a costume?" He caressed the place where her scales transitioned to skin. "Hollywood. She's a Hollywood actress who escaped from filming."

Silas disagreed. "Impossible. She not only looks real. She feels real." He bent down and ran his hand along her scales and squeezed her breast. I lunged for him.

Pavel grabbed me. Moments later, Reht brought Elias on deck. Elias' eyes widened when he saw Ariella. I gritted my teeth. If there was one positive element that came out of this whole thing, it would be that Elias would believe that I was a merrow. Or at least *once* was a merrow.

"What is she worth to Akhbar?" Silas asked Elias and me.

"I..." Elias turned to me as if I could help.

"C'mon, you, don't tell me you didn't know. This is all part of Akhbar's plan, isn't it? And I bet you wanted to find one like this too. Didn't ya?"

"No..."

"Ah, quit with the bullshit." Silas whipped Elias across the side of his head with his gun. "What are they worth?"

Elias spit blood out of his mouth and glared up at him. "Priceless."

Silas whiskered mouth split into a big grin. "Priceless." He slurped air and saliva in through his teeth. "Hear that? *Ding, ding, ding.* We have a winner. Better than a prince. El Shabhad, he'd buy them. He could pay."

Reht shook his head. "Let Akhbar decide."

"He sent spies!" Silas shouted. "We can't trust him." He jutted his chin toward Elias. "We'll kill this one and sell the other two."

Sun beat down on my throbbing head. My mouth felt so dry I couldn't swallow. My legs cramped, and my heart ached for Ariella. Everything had fallen apart. I'd come to save Elias. Now I'd failed and my sister's life lay in danger.

I needed to get us back beneath the sea. All of us. Elias had proven that he loved me. In my heart, I knew the story shell was true. I'd gained the love of a human. Now we could both return to the sea just like the story. I needed to make it happen. Silas and his men were land creatures. They wouldn't be able to follow us to the ocean. Even if it meant facing Krenil, I had to get us there.

I lifted my mother's slender bone whistle and blew.

Chapter Thirty-Nine - Delphin

WORRY FOR ARIELLA and Elias tormented me. The human fabrics I wore against my skin felt rough and dry compared to sea-silk. My body and spirit were raw and wounded.

I peered through the tiny hole that led to the deck. Shapes moved outside but it was hard to see what was happening.

With a loud bang, the hatch burst open. Reht glared. "C'mon."

Two new men stood on deck. A small seaplane sat in the distance, bobbing on the water.

They'd filled a rubber lifeboat with seawater and lain Ariella in that. Remains of uneaten fish floated around her, messy and putrid. Ariella lay unconscious, face gray. I blinked back tears. What had they done to her?

"You've killed her!" I shouted.

"Who's he?" asked a tall mean-looking one I'd never seen before.

Silas raised his eyebrows. "He knew your name."

The man and strode over. "Nah. I'm not one to forget a face." He grabbed my chin between his thumb and forefinger. "Not a boy as pretty as this. Who are you?"

I tilted my head up. "I'm Delphin. That's my sister. She's sick; she needs help."

"Your sister?" The man laughed and ambled back over to Ariella. He ran his fingers along her scales. "They're both pretty. But…"

Silas winked at Reht and nodded toward Akhbar. "A good find, yes? Priceless maybe. What do you think?"

"Does she look like Prince Eran?" Akhbar pointed to Ariella and then to me. "Does he?"

Silas swallowed. "No, sir. Better than a prince though, right? Priceless."

Akhbar whipped his gun from beneath his shirt, marched over, and jammed it up beneath Silas' jaw. "I'll be the judge of what's better. I asked you to do a job. You disobeyed. You *failed*." He turned back to the man with a gut that protruded from a black shirt. "Doc. What you got with you?"

"A basic med kit back on the plane."

Silas nodded. "Get it. Examine her."

Doc left and got into a small rubber boat. He buzzed over to the plane. When he returned, he had a black suitcase. He pulled strange silver objects from inside. One object he put into his ears and placed against Ariella's chest.

"Leave her alone!" I struggled against the ropes that bound me to the metal post. Blood flowed from my wrists as the rope dug deep into my flesh.

Doc ignored me. Silas backhanded me. "Quiet!"

Iron filled my mouth.

Akhbar stood next to Doc while he leaned over Ariella, placing the round circular object to various parts of her body while he listened for something.

"Heartbeat is odd. Her heart is in a different position! It's on the right side, not the left. The right side. Imagine that?" The man had big bushy black eyebrows and brown eyes so dark they looked black.

"What about that one, Doc?" Silas pointed to me. "It has no fishtail but show 'em your teeth. They're just like the girl's."

I pressed my lips tight together.

"Show 'em your damn teeth if you don't want your girlfriend hurt," he warned as he took a few steps toward Ariella. I showed my teeth and shut my mouth again.

The man named Doc squinted in the sun. He scratched his hairy belly and walked over. "Let's see again, boy." His breath smelled disgusting. Burnt things and octopus vomit. I showed my teeth again.

"Is he dangerous?" Doc turned to Silas. "I'd like to examine him too."

"Hold his arms," Silas told Reht. Reht forced my arms behind my back.

Doc poked and probed me. He shoved an object in my mouth. It beeped, and he took it out. He placed the strange circular object against my bare chest. It was cold.

"Same heart placement as the girl." Doc turned to Akhbar. "Interesting. *Very* interesting. What the kid said is true. To the right people, these two are priceless."

"So this is good, yes? We have our deal?" Silas asked.

"You'll get paid when you follow orders!" Akhbar said. "I asked for a prince. This is no prince."

Doc shook his head and whispered, "That's something else. An actual mermaid. A real-life mermaid."

Ariella moaned.

"Let me closer." I struggled forward. "I can help her."

"No," Silas said.

As the sun's angle changed, I got a better view of Ariella's condition. I did not like what I saw. Her face had a gray-blue hue. Her breathing appeared shallow.

Doc fussed over her, eyes glittering. "Her heart is getting weaker. Why not let the boy see what he can do? We want to keep our fishy fresh, yes? With my limited supplies, there's not much I can do."

Akhbar shrugged and laughed. "Fresh fish. Yes. True, true, true."

Silas allowed me closer. I rushed to Ariella and put my hands on her cold, bare shoulders.

"Ariella!" I sent. Nothing. "Ariella!" I projected as loud as I could.

What returned was static, worse than static. Gray limbo. Ariella was almost dead.

Chapter Forty - Delphin

"AKHBAR, BE REASONABLE!" Silas pleaded.

"Consider yourself lucky you get to keep that one. He's bound to be worth something with his strange teeth and organs in all the wrong places." Akhbar and Doc lifted Ariella and with Reht's help, hoisted her down into the small rubber boat.

"She's dying!" I shouted, voice hoarse.

"We'll get her help. Don't worry. We won't let our prize fishy die." Akhbar pinched Ariella's cheek.

"Reht—" Silas started. Reht looked up at Silas and then cast his eyes down.

"You have something you want to say?" Akhbar said. Silas shook his head.

I watched, helpless, while they headed out into the choppy blue sea. Silas and Pavel stood at the deck rail grumbling while they loaded Ariella onto the seaplane. Reht brought the rubber boat back, and they tied it up again alongside *The Wolf*. He climbed up a rope ladder and stood on deck, hand shading his eyes. A horrible buzzing filled the air as the seaplane trundled along the water.

"Ariella!" I screamed.

Silas walked over. "Shut the hell up! Things are bad enough without listening to you whine!" He raised his gun and I cringed, my face still throbbing from my earlier beating. The blow never came.

He lowered his gun. "If you're all I'm getting, I guess I better keep you looking as good as possible. And you, traitor!" Silas pointed at Reht.

"What choice did I have?" he said to Silas. "We work for him, remember?"

Silas glared. "Bring the other one over."

Reht dragged Elias over. "Should I kill him? There's nothing special about this one. Just a dirty desert boy."

Silas looked at me and then at Elias. He kicked Elias hard in the stomach. Elias thrashed and dry heaved.

"Stop it! If you hurt him, I'll, I'll—" My mind whirred through options. What would I do? "I'll kill myself and then you'll have nothing!"

Silas sneered. "You sound like his girlfriend. We won't kill him *yet*. Not as long as you cooperate."

The buzzing continued as the plane circled around the boat and gathered speed.

Ariella belonged to the water. It felt surreal to watch her being taken by the giant mechanical bird. The seaplane they called it. Silas put his hand in front of his eyes to shade it from the glare. Reht stood by him, hands on his hips, legs splayed.

"This one better be worth at least a quarter what his friend is worth." Silas glanced at me as he spit and shouted over the noise as the plane rose above the water.

"They said priceless," Reht reminded him. "What's a quarter of priceless?"

Silas laughed and nodded. "True. Maybe we did okay after all?"

If I hadn't been so frightened, sad, and desperate, I might have found it beautiful. Drops of silver seawater fell from beneath the plane's propellers as it took off above the shimmering gold and silver water. It hung low for a moment and then rose toward the sky in a graceful arc. Its red and blue wings arced to the side

Ariella! A wave of sadness and grief hit me so hard that I sunk to my knees. When I looked up again, it happened. A silver flash burst from the water.

A trident?

It pierced the nose of the airplane and the giant bird's beak exploded in a cacophony of grinding metal. It pitched forward and tumbled to the glittering sea.

Chapter Forty-One - Ariella

WHEN ARIELLA WOKE up, the world buzzed and vibrated around her. What made that horrible noise? An acrid taste filled her nose. Her eyes fluttered open.

She sloshed at the bottom of a plastic tub. Two men sat hunched in a small compartment in front of her. Through the windows, she didn't see the water. Only the blue sky. Her little tub swayed and a wave of nausea washed over her as the horizon tilted at a sickening angle.

Ariella had read about this. She was flying.

Chapter Forty-Two - Delphin

SILAS AND REHT ran to the side of the boat. For a moment, they stood, stunned. Then Silas whirled into action.

He clasped his hands in front of his chest and glanced up at the sky. "God is good. Untie the Zodiac. Let's get over there quickly. Before she sinks."

One of the seaplane's wings had torn half off and lay submerged. Black smoke billowed from the contraption's beak.

Silas and Reht buzzed over in their tiny boat. When they arrived, Silas hopped off onto one of the smoking craft's pontoons. A moment later, he reappeared with Ariella slung over his shoulder.

He placed her in the boat. They maneuvered back a considerable distance and Reht began shooting at the airplane. With a whoosh and a bang, the plane erupted in a massive explosion of fire like I'd never seen.

When I opened my eyes again, they zoomed back toward us, Ariella lying motionless at the bottom of the small rubber boat.

Reht tied up to *The Wolf*. "Pavel, get down here and help us carry her!" he shouted.

Pavel leaned over the side and lowered a rope. The three of them lifted her up toward *The Wolf*. Suddenly, a hand shot from the water, grabbed Pavel's ankle, and yanked him overboard. Ariella fell back into the bottom of the boat with a wet splat.

A face I recognized appeared: Krenil. He grabbed Reht's long hair. Reht shouted.

Silas aimed and fired but missed. Krenil sunk back into the water, dragging Reht with him.

Silas shot into the water over-and-over, eyes wide with fear. Ariella's eyes fluttered open. For the first time since I'd seen her, she appeared aware of her surroundings.

Silas shot until his gun clicked empty. Three merrow lunged and attacked the boat. Silas disappeared in a plume of red blood.

Krenil rose to the surface. He glanced over at *The Wolf*. I'm not sure if he could see me from his vantage, but a chill went up my spine. How little I'd ended up knowing about the merman. It embarrassed me that I'd trusted him all those years. How could I have been that naïve?

With a shout of glee that sent a shiver up my spine, Krenil grabbed Ariella's fin. Her eyes flashed with rage. She arched her back and rotated her fin ninety degrees, whacking him off the boat. He plunged into the water and Ariella fell with him.

"Ariella!" I shouted. Water licked the metal hull of *The Wolf*. A lonesome bird flew over far above. Otherwise, silence. No clues as to what battle might rage beneath the sea.

"Delphin! Help me!" Ariella grabbed at the rope ladder that led out of the water onto *The Wolf*. I struggled against my bonds but couldn't get free.

"I'm trying!"

She tried to pull herself up. Her hands slipped. With a bang, the hatch flew open. Elias stood, stunned.

"I did it!" He pumped his fist into the air.

"Elias! My sister. Help her!"

Ariella flopped and floundered, trying to crawl up the rope ladder that led from the rubber boat. Elias ran to her and helped.

"Now pull up this contraption!" Ariella shouted. "Before the others come."

Elias looked down at the sea. "Others?" he said bewildered.

"Just do it!" I shouted. Elias pulled up the ladder just as a hand grabbed at the bottom rung... and missed. I heard the sounds of tridents banging against the hull.

Elias peered over the side. "Holy crap."

Chapter Forty-Three - Delphin

THE FIRST GOLDEN ray of sun glinted across a flat, blue ocean. *The Wolf* lay silent without the crew. Ominous. It was a large craft meant to be tended by several. Now there were only me, Elias, and Ariella, who wasn't able to help.

Ariella explained that they'd fed her something. Not food— something very bitter. It had poison in it that made her ill but now she seemed fine.

"It doesn't bother you to be out of the water for so long?" I asked her again.

"I'm tired. I'd rather be in the water. But not with Krenil nearby. This is the safest place until we figure out what to do."

I nodded. "I'm going back beneath the sea with you. Elias will come too."

I watched as he surveyed the horizon from the boat's stern, his strong shoulders silhouetted against crimson.

Ariella smiled. "He's fallen in love with you, this human boy? Just like you said." She chuckled. "Trust my brother."

I nodded. "He has, I think. How do you know when a human loves you?"

"I have no experience with humans. Perhaps you might just ask him?"

"You're right." I sighed. "I need to ask and make certain."

* * *

Elias walked to the rail and stood next to me, his full, red lips cracked from days of little water and much sun. "We need to get *The Wolf* running."

I nodded. However, I knew nothing about boats. This morning, I'd gone to the engine room with him, but the stench of metal and fuel nauseated me. We needed to evade Krenil and return to the sea.

"Maybe it's an electrical problem. C'mon."

I followed him to the cabin. The room reeked of sweat and cigarette smoke. Elias leaned over the controls, fiddling with the throttle. I watched as the minutes ticked by. Did Elias love me enough to leave the human world?

As I watched Elias, his hair kept falling in front of his handsome eyes, one brown, one green. His calves looked strong and solid below his cut-offs. I loved him. If Elias loved me half as much, maybe even that would be enough for it to work?

I laid my hand on Elias' back and stroked my hand down to the top of his buttocks. Elias raised an eyebrow.

"You're distracting me." He said it with a smile and a laugh. Hope bubbled in my chest. I grabbed his hand.

"We don't need to fix the boat," I said. "There's another way."

Elias' eyes crinkled in a smile. "Not having much luck so far. I'm listening."

"Come with me and Ariella. Back to where I was born. The sea."

Elias' smile faded, and he dropped my hands. "We don't have time for jokes."

"I'm not joking. I'm serious," I said. "Everything I've told you is true. You've seen my sister."

Elias swallowed and nodded. Then he turned back to *The Wolf's* controls.

I grabbed him. "C'mon. You need to listen to me!" I brushed Elias' hair from his eyes. Then I tried to kiss him. He stopped me.

"Why won't you kiss me?"

"Why the hell do we need to kiss?" He threw his hands up in frustration. "We might die out here!"

"Did you kiss Timu?"

Elias' face turned red. "Are you kidding? Never. No."

"Do you love me?"

"Love you? C'mon, this isn't the time…"

"It takes two seconds to answer! Do you love me or not?"

"You saved my life." Elias looked into my eyes. "I'll never forget that. People say they love each other all the time and it means nothing."

"You saved my life too."

145

Elias shrugged. "Not really…"

"We're even. A life for a life. That's not the question. Do you love me?"

"What does it matter? We have important things to worry about. What does that even mean?"

Anger burned my stomach but I swallowed it back down. "Of course, it matters! It means… that you want to come with me and Ariella. Wherever that might be. That we'll stay together forever. No matter what."

Elias let out a dry laugh and stopped when he saw the sad look on my face. "This day keeps getting more bizarre. Are you proposing?"

"Proposing…" I understood most words through the weird osmosis that had taken place that allowed me to understand Arabic, but sometimes the usage of certain words was difficult.

He raised his eyebrows and his eyes danced with light. "Are you asking me to marry you?"

"Ah." I nodded and smiled. "Yes! Will you marry me?"

Elias' face stiffened. He closed his eyes, sighed, and opened them again. "C'mon, can we *please* stay focused?"

"I am focused!" Something inside me snapped. "I asked an easy question. Do you love me or not?"

"C'mon!" Elias shouted. "Being with you feels good. Like it did with Timu. But love you? *Marry* you? No. That's crazy. We barely know each other. We'll *die* here if we don't figure something out. A real solution."

Tears overflowed my eyes and their sea-salt taste wet my lips. Elias blushed when he saw me crying. I didn't care. I wept, allowing my heart to fill and overflow.

"I know you, Elias. I know your heart and your soul. You know mine too, even if you're not ready to believe it."

"Hey, quit it." Elias put his hand on my shoulder. "I—"

Clanking at the side of the boat stopped us. Krenil's face peeked over the deck edge, teeth bared. His bloodshot eyes filled with rage when he saw me.

Elias fumbled for the gun he'd tucked in his waistband, aimed, and fired.

Chapter Forty-Four - Delphin

WHEN ELIAS FIRED the gun, Krenil disappeared. I ran to the side of the boat.

"He crawled up the anchor chain. C'mon, reel it in!" Elias shouted. We hauled the anchor until it withdrew back inside the vessel.

"How far can they jump?" Elias asked.

"Jump? I'm not certain. Not all the way to the deck, I don't think."

"Not sure if I hit him or not." Elias said.

"I don't see any blood in the water." I cocked my head to the side. Again the silence fell. I heard nothing but the music of Elias' breath and my heart.

"Here." Elias handed me a second gun.

"I don't know how."

Elias took my hand and wrapped my fingers around the weapon. "Aim. Pull."

"What's going on?" Ariella said.

I ran to her.

"Krenil. He climbed up the anchor chain. Elias shot at him."

"Did he get him?"

I glanced toward Elias who stood, gun aimed at the water.

"I don't think so," I whispered.

Metallic clanging pierced the silence. First one, then another and another. Bang, bang, bang. Over and over again. Vibrations traveled up through my feet.

"What are they doing?" Elias shouted.

"Hunting. Attacking with their tridents," Ariella said. "Trying to sink us."

"The hull is too strong," I said. Then I turned to Elias. "Right?"

He shrugged. "How am I supposed to know?"

We looked at each other and clambered down the metal ladder to the hold had once been our prison. The noise was deafening. I covered my ears.

Our feet vibrated beneath us. They seemed to concentrate on one specific spot. Elias crouched down, stroked his fingers, and raised them toward me. They sparkled with water.

From up on deck, the noise wasn't as loud, but now that I'd seen the harm they were doing, each bang made me cringe.

Back on deck, Elias took one of the larger guns and aimed toward the water. With a horrible *rat tat tat*, he shot down, blind until the weapon clicked. The banging stopped.

Leaning over the rail, I peered down into the blue waters. I caught glimpses of motion but couldn't see what was happening. A breeze whistled past my ears. Water lapped at the sides of *The Wolf*.

The sun had barely moved in the sky before the thumping started again. Elias showed me how to fire a pistol. Soon the sun had slid farther down toward the ocean and my fingers were cramped from shooting into the waters. Each time, the same thing happened. We fired several rounds. The banging stopped.

You are useless. Weak. You betray your own kind.

I scanned the water. Though I saw nothing I heard Krenil's voice in my head. Then the scraping and banging started again.

I leaned the gun over the rail, closed my eyes, and pulled the trigger. Nothing. I walked to the other side of the boat where Elias fired his gun into the water. Unlike me, he kept his eyes open, hand darting from wave-to-wave as he aimed at our hidden enemies.

"It needs reloading." I handed it to him. He took it from me.

Elias went down into the hold. When he came back, his face was glum. "There's two inches of water in there. We have one box of ammo left. They will sink us."

Chapter Forty-Five - Delphin

NONE OF US slept that night. With the anchor up, *The Wolf* drifted beneath a sky full of pinpoint stars. My hand was cramped from shooting. I lay beside Ariella. Elias stayed up to keep watch.

Every time I put my head down, the clang of tridents reverberating through the hull woke me. Their incessant drumbeat slowed but never stopped. This was what they were trained to do. *The Hunt.* I never imagined I'd become one of their prey.

Gentle rain on my face woke me in the morning. Feeling the wetness reminded me of home. I rubbed my eyes. Land loomed through the mist. Elias lay slumped in the foredeck. Even the rain hadn't woken him.

"Elias!" I stroked back his wet hair.

He jumped up, fists balled, dark circles beneath his eyes.

"It's okay. Look." I pointed. It was the island where I'd first found him.

I expected him to be excited. Instead, he groaned. "I almost died on that damn island."

"C'mon." I grabbed his arm and took him to the cabin. Silas' keys still lay on the floor where he'd dropped them. I recognized the ring.

"They have supplies on the island. Boxes and boxes of stuff. Weapons."

Suddenly, there was a massive crunch, and we got thrown forward. *The Wolf* groaned and squealed as it scraped against the shallows.

Chapter Forty-Six - Delphin

I SLID ONTO the deck now slick with rain.

"What happened?" Rain glittered in Ariella's eyelashes. "Gosh, this feels nice." Droplets of water ran from her hair down her face and neck.

My eyes darted to the blue-black water that surrounded us. "We hit rocks."

Elias ran to the prow. "We're at the edge of the shallows." He ran down into the hold.

The merrow had stopped their attack. But here in the shallows, I could see the shadowy shapes of merrow flitting in the gray dawn.

When Elias returned, he had bad news. "There's more water in the hold. The damage they did plus the rocks ruptured a seam. We should head for the island."

Behind us, I caught the flash of fins. "How will we make it? They'll attack."

Elias nodded. "We need to distract them. But with only a few bullets left, I don't know how."

"Distract them. Right," I said. "I'll do it. I'm a fast swimmer. I'll distract them while you get Ariella to shore."

Ariella erupted. "Delphin, have you forgotten something? You *were* a fast swimmer. Now you have no fin! They would impale you on their tridents in an instant. You saw what happened to those horrible men." She gestured toward the rubber boat Reht and Silas returned in, now drifting from its line.

Blood rushed to my face. How easily I forgot that I was no longer a water creature. But she gave me an idea.

"Yes! The boat. That's how we'll distract them."

Elias frowned. "Three of us will weigh her down. It would be too slow."

"True. But I have a plan."

* * *

We dragged the small rubber boat close to *The Wolf*. Elias pointed his gun at the water while I rolled down the rope ladder and descended. At any moment, I expect hands to grab me. To hear the zing of bullets.

When Elias gave the sign—a "thumbs-up" he called it—I pulled the cord once, twice, three times just like Elias instructed. The little boat's engine screamed and howled. I took the knife and on his count cut the lines.

The boat tore off into the distance and headed for the open seas. For a moment, nothing happened, then streaks of blue-green followed behind.

We lowered Ariella into the water. Ariella dashed beneath the surface. A pang of regret stabbed my gut as Elias and I trundled our legs and arms forward as fast as we could.

The tide was out so Ariella wasn't able to swim as close to the island as I had when I'd helped Elias. She waited for us, impatient. We'd need to carry her the rest of the way.

"One, two, three!" Elias grunted as we lifted Ariella. "You aren't light, you know that?"

Ariella folded her arms and scowled.

Several times, we almost lost our footing on the slick rocks.

"Don't you dare drop me!" Ariella shouted.

"We have to hurry!" Every step ahead made it less likely Krenil or his gang could follow. It wouldn't be easy to swim through the shallow rock-strewn waters that surrounded the island. The tide rushed in, swirling over our feet and calves. We had to be quick.

Soon, we stumbled onto the rocky shore.

We carried Ariella up the rocky beach to a saltwater grotto and laid her down

"Well, this is better than sitting in stale saltwater on the boat. But not by much," she said.

Elias kicked a stone and sent it rolling down the incline back toward the beach. "This damn island. I can't believe I'm back here. No food, no water!"

"We'll eat fish," Ariella said.

The rain stopped. I walked out of the grotto. Early rays of sun pierced the clouds, turning the water as blue as sapphire. Rocks jutted haphazardly from the shore like the island's teeth. For a moment, a burst of hope flooded my heart. Had we lost them? Maybe Krenil went home? Then I spotted it.

A fin slashed out of the water, then a head. I couldn't see who it was from here. Whoever it was looked up, and I felt eyes meet mine. I stumbled back away from the shoreline.

* * *

Over the next few hours, we managed to turn the island into, if not a home, at least somewhere we could survive for the time being. I caught fish in the shallows. The area swarmed with them.

Just after sunset, Elias finally managed to start a fire. I'd never seen one before.

"Watch it!" Elias warned as I put my hand close just as it emitted a giant *pop!* and orange sparks flew up into the black sky.

Ariella lay and watched from a safe distance. "I don't like it. It's drying out my fin." While Elias worked on dinner, I covered Ariella in cool, wet sand, which seemed to make her more comfortable.

"The first three are ready." Elias gestured toward his feast. He handed me a fish wrapped in a large green leaf. I took a sniff. It smelled odd. The smoky fire had stripped away most of the delicious fish odors. He'd removed the insides, which were the tastiest and most nutritious parts. Maybe those bits got saved for last?

Ariella took a cautious bite and spit a mouthful out in the sand. "Horrible!" Ariella wasn't one to hold back. "It makes my mouth hot and tastes like death."

Elias paused mid-bite and sniffed. "Well, it's cooked. Of course, it's hot. Let it cool. I thought it turned out quite tasty, given the circumstances."

I didn't want to hurt Elias' feelings so I forced myself to eat some while he watched. Finally, I couldn't keep from gagging.

Elias threw up his arms. "Fine, okay, okay if you don't like my cooking, you make dinner next time." He turned away and continued to eat.

Beside Elias sat a blue plastic bucket of tasty, fresh-caught fish. Despite the fire, I could smell them, sitting wanting to be eaten. I snuck behind him, grabbed one for me and tossed a second to Ariella.

I sat back down by the fire. *Delicious.* My sharp teeth ravaged the tender flesh. Cold, fresh, and stuffed full of juicy innards.

When I paused to glance up, Elias sat watching. I couldn't read his expression.

Elias whistled. "Wow. There should be a law against watching you eat."

I blushed. True enough, I had an extremely healthy appetite—it's a sign of virility. It made me feel somewhat bashful to have it pointed out. Ariella grinned and winked at me as she motioned toward Elias. My chest puffed out.

"There's no law, Elias," I flirted. "Watch as much as you like." I looked him straight in the eye as I ripped off the head with my sharp teeth and managed to consume it whole, wiping scales from my lips. He swallowed and turned away, no doubt overcome with desire.

* * *

Rain came that night. Elias collected water in two plastic drums. Our hideaway was no paradise. We monitored the shore in shifts. When the tide came in, Krenil and his gang tried to launch an attack. We found several boxes of bullets and managed to keep them at bay. Even still, the bullets wouldn't last forever.

Our moral diminished. Elias pointed out that our situation was not secure. "The water will dry up. Or if it doesn't, one day it will rain at night during high tide. How will we watch for them then?"

I pointed up at the cliff. "Let's stay up there. At the cave. There's no way they'll be able to crawl that far from the water."

Elias gazed out at the choppy water. "I need to get back on the boat."

"How will it help to get back to the boat? It's too dangerous."

"We came here for food and more ammo. We have ammo. We have food. Best yet, we have a battery! I can radio for help. That is unless they sink the whole damn boat first. I've got to get back before they destroy it and ruin our best chance for rescue!"

I hadn't heard or seen any evidence that they'd done anything to the boat since we landed. Elias didn't understand that a boat without humans onboard was about as interesting as a clamshell without its occupant. On the other hand, I saw his point. We needed to take action. Even if being in air didn't harm Ariella, every morning she threatened she might die of boredom.

Chapter Forty-Seven - Delphin

"I WANT TO go back to the sea, Delphin! You have your walking sticks. You don't understand what it's like to just lie here day after day!" Ariella grew crankier by the moment. Water dripped from the cave ceiling. Outside the air felt dry, in here it felt warm, moist, and humid.

"I know that. Elias wants to get back to the boat to call for help."

"Call for help to who?" Ariella glanced at me.

"Humans."

"No!" Ariella looked at me in horror. "You can't let him. You'd be fine but who knows what humans might do to me? I'd end up on another plane poked by horrible men."

I put my hand on her arm. "Yes. You're right."

"I thought you were bringing Elias back to the sea?"

Shutting my eyes, I hung my head. "No. He doesn't love me. It won't work."

Ariella's eyes glistened with sympathy. "He doesn't love you? But that's impossible. What a fool!"

I laughed. "Perhaps not. After everything I've done, I wouldn't love me either, I don't think."

"You saved his life!"

"I killed his family," I whispered.

"Is that what you told him?"

I shook my head.

"Good. Because it's not true. *They* did that. Not you!"

"Even so." Lying down next to her, I rested my head on her shoulder. "I'll find a way to get you back to the sea, Ariella. I won't let Krenil or anyone harm you. But I may need to stay on land after all."

"Brother, there must be a way. Are you certain he doesn't love you?"

Footsteps crunched on stone outside the cave opening. Elias entered, rubbing his eyes as they adjusted to the dark. "What are you arguing about?"

"Nothing!" we said at the same instant.

"I'll make a run for it at low tide while you distract them from shore. I'll carry over what we need bit-by-bit. I've got to get the radio working."

"You can't," I said.

Elias looked at me strangely. "Can't? Why? If I go at just the right time and you make a commotion…"

"Elias, if you radio for help, horrible people will come and take Ariella away! We need to get her back to the sea."

Elias ran his fingers through his hair. "It's been days! We can't stay here forever. Those men were criminals. Other people won't treat her like that."

"Oh, I bet they will!" she said. "Maybe worse!"

I grabbed Elias' arm. It felt strong and warm beneath my fingers. "Please. I have an idea. Give me a chance."

"I'm listening." He looked into my eyes and I saw trust there. I wished I could say I saw love too. But I no longer understood what it meant for humans to love.

I grabbed the sheath now with its knife and headed to the entrance of the cave. Far down below the water sparkled, beckoning.

"I need to kill Krenil. It's the only way we'll survive."

* * *

Standing at the shore knee-deep in water, I braced myself. I had the knife. Okay, it was much smaller than the tridents, but it held power. I wasn't defenseless.

"Delphin, it's too dangerous. I'll keep Ariella safe when people come, I promise."

I glanced back at Elias. "No doubt you'd try. But how would we know if we can trust humans?"

Elias opened his mouth and shut it. "We won't. Not for sure. But it's our best chance."

I nodded. "I understand. If I can get rid of Krenil, Ariella can return to our pod. My uncle will keep her safe there. Then humans can come. Okay?"

I waded deeper. Soon I walked past the rocks, shoulder depth then up to my neck. The surface of the water disappeared, and I swam.

A school of green and black angelfish scattered into a grove of seaweed. I listened for unusual noises, sent out a gentle pulse of echolocation—several starfish and a school of needle noses—nothing dangerous. When I'd seen Krenil and his crew last, they were lurking around our wrecked boat. I swam beneath *The Wolf.*

The shallows began and ended abruptly. One moment I swam over rocks so low they almost scraped my belly. A few feet farther and the bottom dropped away into sandy blackness.

They came from below. I forgot how quick merrow were. I forgot how slow I'd become. They circled, laughing and jeering.

"You're about as fast as a sea slug now!" Finner said.

I held the knife up, hand shaking. I'd hoped to ambush them if they still lurked in the area. Instead, they'd ambushed me.

"Give me the knife!" Krenil said. "Return what is mine."

Finner lunged toward me. I slashed at him and he jerked back. "Little warrior, huh?"

Suddenly, a blur of blue-green flashed past. Tango! He circled around the barnacle-covered hull of the boat, chattering, happy to see me.

"Give the knife here!" Krenil shouted. "Final request!"

I wasn't sure what Krenil wanted to do with it. Back in the pod, I knew the knife was integral to his sacrifices to the Tentacle Lord.

"Tango!" Tango swam over and circled around me. When he got close, I took hold of his fin. He chattered with glee. Then he pulled me along with him, just like the game we used to play ages ago. Now this game might save my life.

I lengthened my body and tucked my legs together, hoping to reduce drag. We rocketed through the water. It felt so good to move at proper speed! How I missed my fin.

Finner and Teomath followed. Meanwhile, Tango bubbled with excitement. There was nothing he loved more than a good chase! If only he understood the stakes.

His powerful muscles rippled beneath my arms. He zoomed through the crystal blue water then zig-zagged, left, right, up, down. He threw up a cloud of sediment with his nose. It helped obscure us but I knew he was actually searching for clams.

"Please don't find a big juicy one. Not now!" I begged. When it came to food though, he'd never listened to me. Not even once. Lucky for me, this particular area held nothing tasty. Now he zoomed full speed toward a massive wall of coral. I hung on and put my trust in him.

"What the hell are they doing?" Teomath shouted from farther back. I'd learned to never underestimate Tango's ability to confuse merrow with his antics. No doubt they made perfect sense in his dolphin mind.

At the last minute, Tango darted through a narrow passage and into a large, dead area filled with brown sediment. Beyond it lay a grove of thick seaweed. We rocketed inside and soon swam hidden amongst an underwater forest of green. I glanced back. We'd lost them.

Delphin tickled me under my armpit with his snout. I patted his flank, laughing. "Thank you, friend."

Then my hand flew to my waist and the moment of happiness curdled. The knife and its sheath were gone.

Chapter Forty-Eight - Ariella

THE LIGHT OF a full moon shone through the cave entrance. Ariella lay gazing at the velvet black sky. Night was her favorite time. Cool breezes soothed her skin and reminded her of the balmy sea. Footsteps crunched on gravel on the path that led to the cave entrance and then stopped.

"Delphin?" Ariella called out. No answer. Another few steps. "Elias?"

A long shadow appeared. Naked, Krenil hobbled into view. Seaweed clung to his chest, broken shells tinkled in his matted gray hair. And he had legs!

A sly smile crept up his face when he saw her. Ariella's heart rate quickened. To see Delphin with legs was strange, perhaps a little unnerving. Seeing Krenil with legs filled her with terror.

"You, you have legs! But how—"

A glint of light on metal caught her eye. The knife hung at his belt.

"You gave up your legs to get to me? You're a fool!" Ariella cried.

"Temporary," he said. "I will get my fin back, thanks to you. Delphin isn't the only one who learned from story shells."

"Where's Delphin? What did you do to him?"

"Dead. Or will be soon." Krenil smiled.

"I'll never love you!" she shouted. "You'll *never* be able to return to the sea. You evil old fool."

Krenil shook his head. "Don't you understand, Ariella? I love *you*. That's the important part of the story you've missed. I will return to the sea. You will die. Unless you've reconsidered? We'd have a comfortable life together, you and I." A wistful smile formed on his face. "I've watched you grow up and become a beautiful young mermaid. No one knows you better than I. Sometimes though, we overlook and under-appreciate those who are right in front of us."

Ariella wasn't sure if he was joking or had gone mad. Did he think love could be manufactured like plaster? She'd never love this foul, blinking, perverted man.

"If I die, so be it. I've never loved you and never will. In fact, I loathe you."

His smile faded and his mouth puckered together and trembled. "You poor broken thing." He wiped sweat from his forehead. "You don't know how to love anyone. I see now."

Face pale, Krenil stepped toward her. Ariella recoiled and rolled to the side, evading his long fingers. She rolled back inside the cave closer to the cache of weapons. Her hands scrabbled against one of the metal trunks. She pulled herself up, reaching inside. Ariella felt a carton of bullets. That wouldn't help. Desperate, she searched for something sharp.

Feet stomped in front of her and Krenil slammed the lid down, crushing her fingers. She shrieked in pain and fell to the floor.

"Oh no, no." He snatched a coil of rope that sat on one of the chests, yanked her hands behind her back, and bound them tight.

"Help!"

He hoisted her up like a sack of stones and tossed her over his bony shoulder.

Draped over him, screaming, Ariella thrust the edges of her fin down. Sharp fin met soft belly.

He howled and almost dropped her but managed to steady himself and carry her from the cave.

"Delphin! Elias!" she shouted.

Krenil walked to the cliff edge while Ariella struggled and fought to escape.

"No! Stop. You can't."

Krenil laughed. "I can."

Holding her tight, he jumped from the ledge. They plummeted toward the water.

Chapter Forty-Nine - Elias

SINCE TAKING REFUGE on the island, a whole slew of emotions had overtaken Elias. He missed his family. He worried for his mother and Nijah.

Meanwhile, his world had shifted in strange and unexpected directions. Mermen existed, mermaids too. Elias needed to get them all off this island, or they'd die.

He didn't want anything to happen to Ariella. Humans could not be trusted. True. On that, he agreed with Delphin. He wasn't sure what might happen to Ariella if and when the authorities saw her. They might experiment on her. If the wrong person found her, they would sell her like the pirates did. She was a unique and precious being. Priceless.

The mermen trying to harm them needed to be dealt with so Ariella could go back to the sea. It needed to happen fast.

What would Timu do? Timu wouldn't stay on the defensive. He'd take action.

Inspiration struck. Perhaps he could lure the merrow closer to shore and shoot them from the beach? Elias would build a driftwood fort close to the high water mark where he could hide. Right now, whoever stood on the beach was visible from the water. What he needed was an element of surprise.

Elias had just started to drag an enormous piece of driftwood closer to the shore when he heard the screams.

Chapter Fifty - Delphin

DRAGGING MYSELF ONTO the rocky shore, I vomited a jet of water. Air raged in my lungs, burning. I pushed myself onto my left knee and then my right.

The spot by my side where the sheath and its knife had once hung felt empty. I glanced out at the sparkling blue sea. Krenil had what he wanted. Now he'd leave us alone, at least I hoped. What would it mean for the pod though? How many innocents would be duped into sacrificing themselves to the Tentacle God?

The Wolf floated where we'd left her. Clear, blue water lapped against her side and there wasn't a merrow fin in sight. I glimpsed Tango chasing a school of minnows. A lump formed in my throat. I squatted down and put my hands in the seawater.

Thank you, my friend. I sent out as hard as I could, hoping he'd sense my love.

Now that the merrow danger appeared to be gone, Elias would want to take the battery and get the boat's radio working. First, I'd find Ariella. I dreaded telling Elias that his precious sheath was lost again. Most important though, I wanted to get Ariella off the island before we involved humans.

I left the stony shore and meandered through the grove of scrub that wound through the rocks to the cliff-side grotto. Halfway, I paused, a wave of nausea hitting me. From here, the sea spread out blue and vast below. Again, I did not see any merrow fins with their characteristic rainbow hues. This gave me the energy to continue.

"Ariella!" I entered the cave. "Krenil stole the knife. I think they've left, we can—" I stopped. Something was wrong. Ariella was gone! Crates lay tipped over. A can of waterproof matches lay strewn on the floor. The stink of sulfur hung in the air and something else.

Krenil.

It wasn't that I could smell him. I could not. My keen sense of smell didn't work in the air. No, I felt him, like a miasma, permeating the silent stones. But how had he gotten up here? It made no sense.

I rushed from the cave and hunted the area with my eyes. Deep gouges and footprints in the sandy dirt led toward the cliff. I ran and almost tumbled over the edge. Beneath me, the sea roiled. The water wasn't calm on this side.

I noticed more scuff marks near the cliff's edge. Had Krenil used the knife on himself to get legs? If so, why?

My heart overflowed with worry. I'd hoped the knife was what Krenil wanted most. It seemed Ariella had been his prime goal.

Elias arrived, out of breath. He grabbed my shoulder. "Delphin! Get away from the edge! What the hell is going on? I heard screams."

"Krenil has legs. He took Ariella." I looked down. Far below, whitecaps slammed against the rocks, sending salt spray in the air.

"Careful!" Elias tried to pull me back from the edge but I squirmed from his grip.

I risked another look down. Waves continued to churn. Would I clear the rocks? I didn't know. The longer I looked, the more scared I became. If Ariella fell here, then I would fall too. I needed to go before Elias talked me out of it or I lost my nerve.

"Don't forget that I love you." I lurched toward the cliff and jumped.

* * *

Falling through air was a terrifying sensation. Never in my life had I felt less substantial and more fragile. Water hit my body like a hammer, a stone wall, an immovable force. The ever-changing sea could be as hard as bone or as soft as silk. I never realized she could be quite *that* hard though.

When I regained my senses, I followed Ariella's screams. A sliver of optimism tickled my heart. She sounded furious, not terrified. I darted through a grove of spiny coral. Spire after spire rose around me like magnificent purple narwhal horns. I wove through them as fast as I could, cursing my legs.

Soon I arrived at the skeletal remains of an ancient ship. Ariella lay pinned beside one of the vessel's decaying wooden beams, now splintered and algae covered. Finner pulled her hands behind her back, ready to bind her wrists with rusty chains.

Krenil smiled as he held the knife over her heart, trident resting at his side. "Well, my love. It's time."

Jaw clenched with anger, I approached from behind, swimming as fast as my legs would carry me. If Krenil had had his fin, he might have dodged in time. With legs, we were even.

Before Finner and Teomath could react, I grabbed Krenil by his long gray hair and yanked with all my body weight. He held the knife in one hand and the trident in the other. I managed to jab him in his trident hand with the knife.

Blood jetted from a shallow puncture wound. The trident tumbled from his grip in a silver flash. It stuck in the soft, sandy soil beside the ship.

I snatched it. Krenil froze, pulse beating at his throat, wounded hand clutched to his belly. Finner let go of Ariella and circled. When they saw me with Krenil's trident, they paused.

"Kill him!" Krenil's eyes widened with rage.

There was a moment's hesitation. Then they raced toward me. I held my ground. Projecting all my anger, fear, and sadness into the trident, I swam forward.

Chapter Fifty-One - Delphin

KRENIL BARED HIS teeth. He darted behind Finner and Teomath. One of the ship's beams lay propped against the wreckage above. Finner flexed his powerful arms and pushed. It fell, and I dodged just in time. It would have crushed me to death.

A cloud of sediment rose. When it cleared, a clay urn of doubloons had burst open. Shiny disks as bright as tiny suns sat at the sea-bottom.

"Drop it, Delphin. You don't have your magic trident this time." Krenil's knife glimmered in the gloom.

I wasn't sure what Krenil had told them, but I didn't need a special trident.

"You'll never trick me again, Krenil. All I need is a trident that's not a piece of costume junk! A real one. Yours will do fine." Power hummed through its metal. I didn't like Finner. Teomath was a real ass. But I didn't want to harm either of them if I could avoid it.

"Kill him before he strikes!" Krenil shouted.

Finner's eyes flickered with doubt. "Stand down, Delphin."

"Don't talk to him! Kill him! That's an order!" Krenil pounded one of the ship's ribs. The entire structure groaned. He'd crush us all if he wasn't careful.

Then, as if it couldn't get any worse, motion above caught my eye. Elias. He searched the water from above. I looked away quickly, hoping Krenil hadn't noticed. No luck.

Krenil pointed upward. "Delphin loves the human male! Kill him too! Erase the human scourge."

Fear locked my throat. Doubt disappeared from Teomath and Finner's faces. I backed away from the wreckage, hoping to draw them into open water. They swam toward me. I let loose.

You need to learn to control your power.

Uncle Nebulon's words flashed through my head as a blinding pulse of white light traveled through the water and threw me hard against a wall of coral. When I opened my eyes, Teomath lay spasming, holding his chest on the pile of golden disks. Finner and Krenil were gone. I reoriented myself. Ariella was gone too.

My eyes flashed to the surface. Elias swam, legs dangling. I ascended toward him.

Sun beat down on the water. My eyes remained sensitive from the flash my trident attack generated. My chest ached worse than it had in days.

"Delphin!" Elias wrapped his strong, wet arms around me. "Thank god you're okay. What the hell happened down there? There was an explosion."

I grabbed his shoulders. "I'll explain later. They took Ariella. Did you see which way they went?"

Elias nodded. "After the flash, I saw shapes. I wasn't sure who they were. They swam that direction." He pointed perpendicular to the island.

"Get back to shore!" I shouted. "You'll be safest there." I dove back beneath the water. Legs burning, I swam with maddening slowness. My only consolation was that Krenil couldn't go too much faster than me. On the other hand, he had Finner with him, although I could count on Ariella putting up a struggle. I didn't dare alert them to my presence by calling Tango for help. So I continued on my own.

Soon I found them, thanks to Ariella's noise and commotion. I arrived to the sweet sight of Ariella taking a handful of sharp pebbles and throwing them in Krenil's face. Krenil cried out in pain and slashed out blindly with the knife. Ariella dodged back just in time.

Taking advantage of the distraction, I snuck behind Krenil and smashed his right hand. The knife tumbled into the silt. I spun around and pointed the trident at Krenil's chest. I was getting good at this.

"Drop the trident!" I shouted to Finner.

"Why would I do that?" Finner replied.

"Drop it or I'll kill him!"

Confusion furrowed Finner's brow. He'd never been known for his quick wits.

"Kill me if you have the nerve!" Krenil smiled and opened his arms wide.

"I will!" I pushed forward.

The tip of the trident drew a drop of blood. Other than that, nothing happened. Either I'd spent my power or I didn't feel sufficient raw emotion.

My eyes still burned with the afterimage of Teomath. The water had burned bright, then he'd tumbled to the seafloor, clutching at his heart. Images of Barron's look of terror when he died flashed through my mind. And Crusock too. He'd looked surprised when Father's trident impaled his chest. All this death. All this suffering. Did it have to be this way?

My hands shook. Krenil stared at me with dull eyes.

"Well? Go ahead and do it!" Krenil sneered.

Ariella's eyes flashed with anger. "He deserves it, Brother. Don't be scared."

"I'm not scared! I know he deserves it!"

Finner swam closer.

"You! Stay back!" Ariella shouted as she dug for the knife in the sand. Finner froze.

I shook my head, trying to clear whirling images that attacked like sharks. It didn't seem that long ago that Krenil taught us hide-and-seek in the kelp groves or pulled magic treats from behind our ears to encourage us to behave. But he'd betrayed me.

"Did you know that Krenil was the last person to see Mother? Before she went missing." Ariella shot Krenil a look of pure hate.

Krenil chuckled. "You have no proof."

My mind froze. "What are you saying?"

"I must say though, that your mother thought she was too good for me. Like you, Ariella."

Anger flooded my body. I steadied the trident and was about to jab Krenil through the stomach when a familiar but unexpected voice shattered the spell.

Chapter Fifty-Two - Delphin

"MY, MY, MY!" Uncle Nebulon swam into the grotto, trident in hand. "My nephew managed to snatch your own trident, Krenil? Tsk Tsk. I thought you were a more proficient warrior than that. Can you remind me what the penalty is for losing one's trident in battle? Is it death or dismemberment? I get so confused by all the rules…"

"He cheated! Sheer luck!" Krenil barked.

"Back up, Delphin." Uncle Nebulon gestured at me with his trident.

I froze, too stunned to react.

"Uncle?" Ariella's eyes were wide.

Krenil sneered. "Nebulon, help me remedy these rule breakers and deviants."

My heart grew cold. I thought Uncle Nebulon hated Krenil? Now, they greeted each other like co-conspirators. Ariella looked as confused as me.

Uncle Nebulon smiled. "Your plan with the trident worked well, Krenil. Perhaps too well if a young fry like this bested you?"

Krenil's face turned red, then he returned a sickly smile as he righted himself. "I've been out in open seas for days. A merman gets tired away from home."

"Yes. An old merman. No matter. I'm here now." Nebulon swam closer. "Delphin. Do as I say!" he bellowed, inches from my face. He slammed his trident against mine. It flew into the air. He tossed it back to Krenil.

Ariella's cheeks became mottled with rage. "Uncle, you betrayed us? You've been working with this… this sea louse all this time?"

Krenil laughed. "You're a naïve little fry, aren't you, my Ariella? We both wanted Jahvo dead." He turned to Uncle Nebulon. "You have everything you wanted. Now it's time for what is mine. Give me

Ariella so I can regain my fin. Let me return to the pod to continue my good work."

Uncle Nebulon nodded. "You are right. Now I will give you what is owed." He gestured toward Krenil's trident. "Fight me, win, and you may live. Otherwise, receive the death you deserve. Either way, my niece and nephew will not be harmed. They are not part of this."

Krenil's face whitened. "What? This isn't what we agreed on!" he sputtered.

"Consider yourself lucky I'm giving you the chance to defend yourself in a fair fight. It's more than your pathetic existence warrants."

"Nebulon. Have a heart! I'm old, tired, and wounded." He held out his shaking hands. "I need to return to the pod and rest. I have no time for unnecessary fights."

"Heart? My heart turned to bone when Barron died, Krenil!" Nebulon twirled his trident, preparing for battle. "Ariella, return to our hiding place. Delphin, you're a land creature now. Leave. Both of you."

Neither of us moved. Too much had happened at once. I barely knew up from down.

Nebulon thrust the prongs of his trident toward Krenil's chest. Krenil parried with perfect form, but he was slow. All this time, I thought he'd been showing me various moves at half-speed for my benefit. It seemed he couldn't move any faster. A master of form and technique but no true skill.

"Or fight Finner, if you must!" Krenil countered.

Finner nodded. "I will do as ordered."

"No. This is *our* fight," Nebulon replied. "I've waited years for this."

Krenil's face contorted with anger. "This is against all rules, regulations, and dictates! We had an agreement!"

"Damn you and your rules. Your rules killed Barron!" Uncle Nebulon lunged forward again. His trident glanced Krenil's with a clang. Krenil hid behind Finner, hoping for protection.

"Stand down, Finner!" Nebulon shouted. Finner had a broader chest than Nebulon, was at least twenty years younger, and taught trident skills to all of Father's soldiers. I doubted Nebulon would be a match.

Finner sprang forward and, with two quick swipes of his trident, opened a nasty gash on Uncle's forearm. An evil grin spread across Krenil's face. Uncle Nebulon managed to hang on to his trident, but he faced a serious disadvantage against an armed, highly trained soldier.

"Kill Nebulon first. Then Delphin and Ariella," Krenil commanded.

Finner nodded. He pointed his trident. Uncle Nebulon gritted his teeth.

"Wait!" I shouted. "Finner—you and I have never been friends, but you taught me how to wield a trident, right?"

Finner hesitated.

"Was I your best student?"

Finner sneered. "Easily my worst."

"Yet I dealt the blow that killed my father. Haven't you ever wondered how that was possible?"

"Ignore the boy! Kill them all!" Krenil shouted. Now I had Finner's attention, and the cogs in his brain were churning.

"For months I practiced with a dummy trident."

"True!" Uncle Nebulon shouted. "A complete fake."

"Given to me by Krenil! All that time, I practiced with a useless trident. But the first time I faced Father, I was given a real trident. By who? Krenil! And who manipulated Father into fighting me? Krenil too! He orchestrated the whole thing. He's admitted it to us. He hid my true power from and schemed to unleash it on my father."

"Hmm," Nebulon said. "I like where this is headed."

"It was Krenil who killed Jahvo. He's not a rule keeper. He's a rule-breaker, guilty of treason!"

Ariella swam behind Krenil. His eyes were on me. He didn't see her coming as she swam through the murk.

Silent, she lunged and stabbed Krenil hard through the back. I swam forward, grabbed his trident, and finished the job before he could harm her.

Whorls of dark blood clotted in the water. Krenil tumbled to the seafloor. He took several, raspy breaths. More blood pooled around him. Then he slumped into the sea-sludge, dead.

A single tear bubble popped from my eye. I brushed it away, hoping no one noticed. He deserved no tears from me or anyone.

Finner regarded Krenil's dead body, face impassive. He turned to Uncle Nebulon. His trident remained pointed toward our uncle.

"Well?" Uncle said.

"What you've said raises questions. I'll offer you the benefit of the doubt. For now. When I return to the pod, I'll tell them Krenil is dead. I expect the Council will want a full accounting from all of you." Finner tilted his head at us and swam off into the blue.

Chapter Fifty-Three - Delphin

"YOU WERE WORKING with Krenil?" My transmission quavered with shock.

Uncle Nebulon winced as Ariella pressed sea-floss to his wounded forearm. "Jahvo killed Barron, the love of my life. I vowed justice and revenge. Krenil became my only hope for justice. All along, I never blamed you, Delphin. I blamed your father and Krenil. Their supporters remain strong. Followers of the Tentacle Lord won't be easy to squash. As son and daughter of the Regent, I need you and Ariella by my side to face the council. It will lend legitimacy to our claims."

"So it is possible then?" I swam to him. "To get my fin back?"

Uncle Nebulon nodded.

"What about Elias? If he was willing, could he also gain a fin?"

Uncle Nebulon hesitated. "Perhaps. You must make some difficult choices."

Ariella's eyes flared with anger. "Tell him the whole truth! He loves Elias."

"Do you really love the human boy?" Uncle Nebulon cocked his head.

"Yes. Plus, he has no family. I can't just leave him."

Uncle Nebulon put his uninjured hand on my shoulder. "I'm not saying I condone The Hunts. I do not. But humans are primitive creatures. They don't know how to love. They're limited by their primitive communications. Imagine if all we had were sounds to speak? It addles their brains."

"Elias will love me. He needs more time." A jolt of fear lodged in my chest as I remembered our recent conversation. Love came easily to me. It felt instinctive. Maybe Uncle Nebulon was right about humans? Perhaps they were a bit primitive?

Above me, I spotted a plume of bubbles near the boat. Elias had jumped in for a swim. Wearing a pair of goggles, he waved from above. He appeared intrigued. I gave him a thumbs up and he grinned. He stayed for a while longer, watching from above.

Despite everything he'd seen, perhaps he needed to convince himself: Mermen were real. Mermaids were real. It was not a dream.

"Come back with us, Delphin," Uncle said. "Your... human pet will survive fine on his own." He motioned to Elias. "Just as your dolphin did."

"Elias is not my pet."

Uncle frowned. "I refuse to condemn that which I don't understand... and yet the idea of a merrow with a human makes my stomach queasy. Perhaps if you understood what was at stake, you'd consider reason? We need you, Delphin. We can't afford to lose you to the human world. Not even for what you imagine is love."

Ariella's eyes filled with sadness. Her eyelashes fluttered and I thought she'd never looked more beautiful swimming among bubbles that clung to her like silver jewels.

Uncle came closer. "We must return and clean up the mess of a pod Jahvo and Krenil created."

"Are you going to fill him in on what's required, or shall I?" Ariella asked.

"It will muddy his thinking." Uncle waved her off.

"What are you talking about?" I gently probed Ariella's mind. She blocked me and turned away, hands clutched around her stomach as if she might be sick.

"Think of what has been lost already! We can't jeopardize the pod for one human boy! You don't understand the extent of the harm Jahvo and Krenil caused. War had already killed thousands. We're on the brink of extinction. More and more fall under the spell of the Tentacle Lord, polluting their minds."

Ariella wrung her hands. "Yes, Uncle, but there must be another way."

"Fine, Delphin deserves to know all his options. So as I was saying. Ariella discovered some extremely interesting information in those ancient scrolls that Jahvo wanted to destroy. Yes, there is an option for you to regain your tail. It's not a children's story shell though, it's work for a merman and requires a hard decision on your part. Will you commit to coming with us, or will you stay with the human boy?"

Delphin felt the bottom drop from his stomach and fall far down to the ocean floor. This wasn't a decision that he wanted to make, he realized. To choose between Ariella, his sister who he loved more than anyone and who loved him back. Or Elias, who he he'd fallen in love with, felt emotions that he'd never experienced… but who didn't love him in return.

"Well?"

"There is no way to get my fin back. Elias doesn't love me." My jaw tightened as I transmitted it. It hurt to admit but at least it made things straightforward.

"As I said, his love of you is not required," Uncle reminded me.

A fierce wave of protectiveness shot from Ariella's heart to mine. And in that minute, I made my decision. Ariella was my tribe, my one and only sister. Our love flowed back and forth deep between us. Elias was much more complicated. I couldn't stand the thought of losing him. I had to do what was right.

"Once I'm certain Elias is safe with his kind, I'll go back with you, Ariella," I said. "If I can reclaim my tail, I'll do it."

Ariella darted toward Nebulon. "He can't decide without knowing!" The garbled confused transmission flew off her as she hit Uncle with her fists.

"Ariella!" Uncle grabbed her hands.

"Tell me," I said. "What do I need to do?"

"It involves sacrifice."

"He's already sacrificed enough!" Ariella shouted.

"Do you love the human male or is it lust?"

I thought of Elias and my heart surged with warmth. "Yes. I love him."

"Does he love you?"

I shook my head. "I don't know."

"Well, then it's simple, although difficult. Drag the human male to the bottom of the sea on the full moon. Tomorrow night. If he loves you, he will live and become one of us. If not, he will die. Either way, you will regain your fin. That's not unfair, is it?"

I hesitated for a moment as what he said sunk in. "Unfair? That's worse than unfair! He might die!"

"You will *never* be content with a human male. You're young and think you love him. What you feel is not a true love. It can't be. It's impossible."

"How can you know that? You were right when you said your heart turned to bone, Uncle. You're as blind as Krenil and you don't see it."

A sad smile flickered across Nebulon's face as he shrugged. "One day, you'll realize that I'm right. We'll wait for you until sunrise. I hope you'll make the right choice."

Chapter Fifty-Four - Delphin

MIDNIGHT BLUE CLOUDS sliced the sky like knives amid the sparkle of stars but all I managed was a quick glance. I'd have happily given up stars to get the night over with.

Elias found some wine and drank quite a bit. He'd managed to fix the radio and contact authorities on the mainland—somewhere in the European States. Soon people would rescue him, us. Humans. Elias was in a jovial, boisterous mood.

The full moon hung low in the sky, large, brilliant, and white. This human world felt so cold sometimes.

Elias put his arm around me as he gazed up at the sky. "It's such a still night. I wonder what sailors did on nights like these?"

I avoided his gaze. "I know little about sailors." *Except that my pod hunted them.*

"I didn't think you would." Elias put his arm around me and pulled me close. "I'm sorry about the other night." He pressed his hand to my bare chest. "Your heart beats so fast!"

"I'm scared."

We were both shirtless. Elias' ribcage rose and fell as he breathed. "Don't be scared. It's all gonna work out. I'll make us something to eat."

Does Elias feel love for me now? If I moved fast, I could overtake him, drag him to the bottom of the sea, and stab him before any doubts arose. It's not very romantic, but perhaps it would work?

While Elias prepared a makeshift dinner, I stared at the smooth black sea and wanted to vomit.

"C'mon, let's eat. Celebrate!" Elias said. "We survived! I caught fish for us! And I *didn't* cook yours, just how you love it, right?" He grinned.

After dinner, Elias grew drowsy. He leaned against me and let out a series of peaceful snores

A breeze rose. Clouds unfurled in front of the rising moon. Would it storm? I lay Elias back until his bare chest was exposed to the sky.

Choked with emotion, I shut my eyes and put my ear to his chest. His heart *ka-thumped* against my ear with a slow, steady rhythm. Could love be heard like the sea's waves? While the moon sank into the sea, I listened to the music of his breathing and tried as hard as I could to detect the sound of love in the beating of his heart.

"Elias?"

He opened his sleepy eyes, which widened when he saw the knife in my hand.

"This is yours. Take it." I handed it to him.

He held it up in the moonlight. "It's odd to see the blade with its sheath. All my father's life, he wanted it to be complete again. Thank you, Delphin."

We settled back together and looked up at the sky. Elias' hand explored my body. I stirred as he massaged my thigh. I glanced at him. "Elias? Do you love me now?"

Elias bit his lip and smiled. "Again with that?"

His face grew thoughtful, lips quivered, and he shrugged. "We've been through a lot together. Maybe I do? I'm not sure."

"Say it, then."

He sighed gazed up at the stars. "I love you. There, I said it. Now, are you happy?" He turned to me. Three words—those magic three words. I'd heard them with my ears. But I wasn't sure my heart believed him.

When I tried to kiss him, he wavered for a second but pulled away. I sighed.

"Sorry," he said. "It's just—"

"It doesn't matter." I put my finger to his lips and kissed him other places.

Later, Elias lay naked next to me in the balmy night air. I stood on deck scanning the water for signs of Ariella or Uncle Nebulon.

I love you, Elias had said. The stars were our witnesses. But he'd also told me that humans say things they don't mean. How would I know for sure? There were no rules to follow, no regulations to consult. Maybe it would work… or maybe it would fail and he'd die?

It wasn't too late but soon it would be. The knife rested by Elias' side. Seawater rippled against the boat's hull, caressing it in the darkness. Finally, I made my decision. I left Elias and jumped off the side of the boat to tell Ariella and Uncle.

I searched the area. "Ariella? Uncle?" I saw neither of them nor did I sense their presence.

I rolled onto my back, hating the way my legs hung down, leading to an unpleasant roll I hadn't managed to correct. Floating, I watched the night sky put on its show. Still no sign of either of them. I climbed the ladder onto *The Wolf*.

Back on deck, something shiny and white caught my eye. Rushing to the port side, feet burning with the now-familiar pain, I stumbled. I grabbed the object and held it in the moonlight. A conch shell—Ariella's favorite. I held the shell to my heart.

One day, we'll see each other again, Ariella. I'll return to the sea but with Elias! I'll find a way!"

I returned to Elias and found him shivering in the night air. I gathered blankets from below deck and covered him. I burrowed beneath the wool fabric with him. Elias murmured and held me against his naked body. We fell asleep sprawled beneath the black sky.

Chapter Fifty-Five - Delphin

MEN AND WOMEN in uniforms arrived and rescued us as Elias promised. He prepped me on what to say.

They brought us to a small room where they questioned us over and over again. Elias told the truth, except where it came to me. I told them I came from Elias' village and lost my memory after almost drowning.

Elias gave them his mother and sister's names. They had no information. He slumped forward, face in his hands. One day, I had to tell him what I'd witnessed my merrow clan do. Now didn't seem like the right time.

More people came—these ones wore different clothes from the others. They transported us in a strange contraption. Elias called it a van. For two days, they kept us comfortable but confined to a room with bars on its windows and two narrow beds.

With their help, we filled out piles of paperwork that they stamped with giant red marks. They gave us pieces of paper—money—along with instructions to attend a class on something called job skill matching. Then they let us go.

* * *

Hundreds of boats and small ships dotted Adria's harbor. Each vessel attached to a dock that led up to the long pier. Beyond the harbor… a city. A city built on land.

Now we stood, alone in this alien land for the first time. I'd never seen so many people or that many legs! And doing so many unfamiliar things. Handing pieces of money back and forth. Holding odd shiny rectangular objects to their faces or sometimes to their ears.

"How big is this pod?" I asked.

"Millions, I'm sure." Elias gazed around at the bustle and swallowed. "Much bigger than my town."

I stepped forward and stumbled. Elias grabbed me. It had been days, but I still felt as if the surface undulated beneath my feet. As if I walked on water, not land.

"C'mon, let's go." Elias pointed toward a street.

"Where?"

"I dunno. Food first, I guess."

I gulped and nodded. Part of me couldn't wait to learn what life in a land city involved. Another part felt terrified. And I couldn't help worry that every step I took would separate me from the merrow world, perhaps forever. I grabbed Elias' hand. Elias gave me an awkward look and removed his hand from my grasp.

"Elias. If I find a way, will you come back to the sea with me?"

"Return to the sea? We just got here."

"I know. But later."

Elias looked back at the water. "Let's give it some time."

Beyond the harbor, people bustled. Elias asked a man a question, and the man frowned and shook his head.

"Humans aren't friendly," I noted. The man jumped into a blue contraption with wheels. A car, I learned from Elias.

"He didn't speak Arabic," Elias said. "Few will here, but we'll work it out. You seem good with languages… maybe you can pick up Italian?"

I nodded. As an experiment, I reached my mind out to an older woman who brushed my arm as she hurried past. I drew back, bewildered by thousands of foreign impressions. We wandered into a square.

"All food needs to be bought?" I asked, incredulous.

"Unless you catch it yourself." Elias winked. This soothed my mind. I saw no reason why I wouldn't be able to fish. As long as we were near water.

"Let's stay close to the harbor," I suggested.

Elias shrugged. "We can try but we need to find work. Start a life here."

My chest trembled. *Start a life?* I wanted to see how humans lived. But I didn't want to settle here forever. I hoped he wouldn't either.

"If you want to head off on your own, I understand," Elias said, perhaps mistaking my silence for reluctance. I frowned. Once again, I noticed the yawning gap that lay between us.

Each step we took away from the water, my fear grew. I turned and watched a fishing boat arrive.

"C'mon," Elias said. "It's expensive around here. Full of tourists. They gave us vouchers for a youth hostel. We can eat there."

"Will we be able to see the water?" I grabbed Elias' hand.

He glanced at the crowd and pulled his hand away. "Probably not. We'll come back here tomorrow. First thing. I promise."

I steeled myself against the gloomy images and worries that circled like sharks. We kept walking and the next time I turned, there were only buildings. A horrible suffocating feeling welled up inside. The sea was gone. For the first time in my life, I couldn't see her. I couldn't hear her. I couldn't even smell her.

The city was stationary, immobile. The buildings sat with no flow around them except the curious, staccato walking motions of people. The compulsion to run back to the harbor was overwhelming. The farther we walked, the more crowded it got.

"Elias, are there rules here?"

"Rules? Yes. Laws, I suppose."

"Good rules or bad ones?"

"Some of both, I guess. Don't know much about it," Elias admitted.

People and noisy, smoking vehicles rolling on black circles— tires— surrounded us. It was unlike anything I'd ever experienced.

"Is it against the rules for us to hold hands?"

Elias stopped and shrugged, his eyes crinkled in a shy, resigned smile. "Probably not. Would you care if it was?"

"No," I admitted. He took a deep breath and grabbed my hand again. We stood, inches from each other. I wanted to kiss him. Was that against the rules? His rules?

I leaned in and pressed my lips against Elias' warm mouth. For a moment, I expected him to draw away. He didn't. He kissed me back.

My heart thrummed in my throat. Elias' face flushed and his eyes darted to two men walking past. No one seemed to pay any attention.

All my fear floated away. Warmth surged through my chest. For the first time, the air I breathed felt silky, smooth, liquid, and as effortless and easy as water.

"I love you," I said. This time, it didn't matter if Elias said the words back. I felt what I felt. I'd kept him safe. We'd kept each other safe. I'd helped bring him back to land. Maybe we would end up heading our separate ways? If we did, I'd be sad, but I'd survive.

No matter what happened, I'd found love after all. It sat, radiating in my heart. An inextinguishable glow. I was about to continue walking. Elias stopped me.

He took my chin and looked me in the eye. "I love you too, Delphin." His eyes glistened with moisture.

This time, I believed him.

* * *

IF YOU ENJOYED this book, please tell a friend or leave a review on Amazon so that this story can find the right readers! I would be extremely grateful. :-)

Join My V.I.P. List to Get Your Free *Mermaid Curse* Book and be the first to learn about the next book in the series! mskaminsky.com

THE MERMAID CURSE Series

Alabaster Island: The Mermaid Curse Prequel

The Atlantis Twins: Book One

The Atlantis Song: Book Two

The Atlantis Queens: Book Three

The Mermaid Curse Box Set (Book 1-3)

❈ ❈ ❈

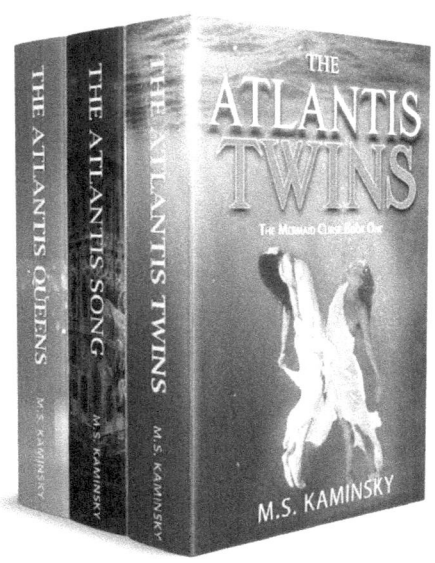

Coming Soon:

Thunder's Rhyme

M.S. KAMINSKY WRITES young adult urban fantasy and sci-fi with dashes of suspense, mystery and romance. His most recent release, The Mermaid Curse Series, reveals the enigmatic origin of mermaids in a gripping fantasy that spans generations of women.

When M.S. is not writing he can be found with his husband attempting to tame the white water rapids of upstate New York or weeding in their garden. So far the rapids (and the weeds) are winning!

M.S. has been a lifelong writer. At four, he dictated his first short story to his dad before his hands were coordinated enough to hold a pencil. Today, his coordination is still questionable. However, his determination to write a good story remains just as strong as that spunky, four-year-old.

Visit www.mskaminsky.com to learn more and grab your free book.

www.ingramcontent.com/pod-product-compliance
Lightning Source LLC
Chambersburg PA
CBHW051957220626
47052CB00004B/982